The Fool

ALSO BY ANNE SERRE

The Governesses

ANNE SERRE

The Fool

and other moral tales

translated from the French
by Mark Hutchinson

A NEW DIRECTIONS PAPERBOOK ORIGINAL

Originally published in French as "Le mat" (Editions Verdier, Paris, 2005), "Le narrateur" (Mercure de France, Paris, 2004), and "Petite table, sois mise!" (Editions Verdier, Paris, 2012). Published by arrangement with Mercure de France, Editions Verdier, and the French Book Office, New York. "The Narrator" was originally published in a longer version: Anne Serre shortened her French text in 2019.

New Directions gratefully acknowledges Christopher Middleton and Ralph Manheim for their translations of the excerpts from Goethe's "Erlkönig" (in "The Fool") and a Grimms' fairy tale (in "The Wishing Table").

First published as New Directions Paperbook 1458 in 2019
Manufactured in the United States of America
New Directions Books are printed on acid-free paper
Design by Erik Rieselbach

Library of Congress Cataloging-in-Publication Data
Names: Serre, Anne, 1960– author. | Hutchinson, Mark, translator.
Title: The fool : and other moral tales / Anne Serre ; translated from the French by Mark Hutchinson.
Description: First New Directions edition. | New York : New Directions Publishing, [2019] | Series: New Directions Paperbook ; 1458 | "A New Directions Paperbook Original" |
Identifiers: LCCN 2019026073 | ISBN 9780811227162 (paperback) | ISBN 9780811227179 (ebook)
Subjects: LCSH: Serre, Anne, 1960– —Translations into English.
Classification: LCC PQ2679.E67335 A2 2019 | DDC 843/.914—dc23
LC record available at https://lccn.loc.gov/2019026073

10 9 8 7 6 5 4 3 2 1

New Directions Books are published for James Laughlin
by New Directions Publishing Corporation
80 Eighth Avenue, New York 10011

CONTENTS

The Fool 3

The Narrator 43

The Wishing Table 105

THE FOOL

I CAME ACROSS THIS LITTLE FIGURE RATHER late in life. Not being familiar with playing cards, still less with the tarot, I was slightly uncomfortable when I first set eyes on him. I believe in magic figures and distrust them. They have powers, of that you can be sure. A color can derail a train, a figure observing you can turn the world upside down.

One day a friend called Michel gave me a tarot pack. Some friends play a peculiar role in your life. You think your friendship is based on certain shared tastes and interests—and there's some truth in that—then you discover—time has to have gone by—that they've sprung up like traffic police on the highway of the imagination, just when you were least expecting them, to hand you a secret package or message, though they themselves know nothing of their role, and you yourself had no idea they were on a mission. You part, and the message slowly deciphered—again, late in the day, since nothing ever happens on time— starts to unwind its coils in you. Ten years later, you examine this tarot pack you have been given, and you see THE FOOL, who gives you quite a start.

For a long time, I had a small statuette in my flat that another friend, Mark, advised me to throw away. There are friends who lead you abruptly to switch roads, friends who save you from disaster: valuing friendship is one of the few things one gets right in life.

When I read the instructions for the tarot (in the booklet that comes with the pack), I felt uneasy and on edge. I don't like esoteric language. Esoteric language is evil, unlike the language of poetry, which has only healing powers. The language of poetry—we know this, but it's worth repeating—is a medicine, and because, like every narrator in the world, I need to look after myself, I take a regular dose.

Reading the little handbook, I couldn't help thinking that the friend who had given me the tarot was much more agile than I was when it came to understanding a language I couldn't make heads or tails of. Michel is the kind of young man who some people think fantastical. I don't. His flights of fancy are woven in a poetic web: he has to work through them, flitting about like a bottle imp — and laughing all the while — before making his way among the more valuable threads of his books. We were on vacation in the Alps with Mark and other friends. It was the summer when Michel was so taken with his tarot pack that girlfriends would call him to find out about their future, and he, on the other end of the line, would play around with his cards, genuinely doing his utmost to reveal their fates. Sometimes he would tell us he had work to do and would go off in his car for a couple of days.

We were walking in the Alps with Mark and had made our way down into a dried-up riverbed. I was picking red flowers, I think. Mark then said something extremely important, which, needless to say, I have forgotten. A phrase like the one Hans Castorp heard one day in the mountains: a farmer was walking by and said to someone, "Good day to you." And it changed Hans Castorp's life.

At the chalet Michel spent the mornings translating *Jerusalem Delivered* on his computer. He had conversations with little Hugh, the son of a friend of ours, who would tell him his dreams over breakfast. Perhaps because Michel was a psychotherapist at the time, he had a way of speaking to little Hugh (who was six or seven) that made me prick up my ears. Personally, I would love to be spoken to like that. We swam in a very cold lake, some of us would go walking in the mountains (I stayed behind at the chalet). I was very fond of the little vegetable plots that the local people had laid out in their enormous meadows, and their way of stacking wood for the winter under a lean-to beside the house. I've always liked things arranged in rows.

I wasn't ready yet to meet THE FOOL. The image of the vagabond was one I'd long been familiar with; it was taking shape, but very slowly. Things need time to take shape, especially if you're burdened with a neurosis. If you're willing to treat it on your own, you can disentangle the threads and advance. But it's slow going. Psychotherapy speeds up the process: but only on condition you don't consent to it in extremis. Then again, you might not like things being picked apart too quickly. You might like desiring something intensely before having the satisfaction of disentangling it all.

It's funny, that little dot in THE FOOL's French name, LE • MAT. The instructions explain that everything in the arcana is important, everything has to be taken into consideration: each little color, each little form or sign. I understand what that means: it's the same in life, where you have to be both extremely vigilant and in a state of intense reverie in order to take in all the clues which later, assembled, examined and studied, will enable you to progress a little. Yet while I'm fairly accustomed to this in life, with the cards I come up against a wall. They arouse no emotions in me. The drawings strike me as crude, the colors ugly. Only death which is never named gives me a little flush of warmth. The hanged man reminds me vaguely of something. He's a fine figure of a young man: hanged, but with an unassuming air, as though he was picking fruit from the tree.

When we were children we used to play Mistigri. And whenever one of us—a cousin, a sister, it may even have been me—found the Jack of Clubs in her hand, she would let out a cry of terror, not in jest but because she was genuinely afraid. When Madame Bovary meets her Mistigri—the blind man at the foot of the hill who blocks the path of the Hirondelle on the road to Yonville—she's terrified. One other figure in particular has always frightened me: that of a young or a grown-up girl, utterly bizarre and abnormal, lying in bed in a Fellini film. I certainly wouldn't write a book about an image that has frightened me. I would try, by writing a book, to reach the point where the terrifying image is canceled out and rendered innocuous.

THE FOOL, for all his peculiarities, is still the tarot figure I'm most familiar with. What's strange is his way of placing the staff his bundle hangs from over his right shoulder while grasping the staff in his left hand. The gymnastics involved are so acrobatic that even in a sentence it's hard to give an account of them: sometimes I place the left hand first, followed by the right shoulder, sometimes the staff first, followed by the bundle, then I switch around, trying a different order without ever finding a proper balance. THE FOOL, to begin with, prevents you from writing properly.

Another peculiarity: an animal is standing behind him, but you would be hard pressed to say if it's a dog, a cat, a fox, a hyena or a chimera. To crown it all, this nameless animal is the same hideous flesh color as THE FOOL's dangling bundle, which it's trying to reach. If he didn't have his animal, THE FOOL would be a bit lonely treading the desolate earth (I screen out the animal with my hand and find that something is lacking to make THE FOOL THE FOOL). Apart from that, he's wearing a cap and bells, which comes as a surprise to no one, and the way he holds the staff from which his bundle hangs, with the extraordinary gymnastics this entails, is similar to the way one holds a flute.

He reminds me of Hamelin and the Pied Piper, the man who leads a whole town to its death. But where did I read that? My memories are truncated and deformed, they always contain an error. To console me, some people, especially Mark, tell me that's why I write fiction. But it worries me, as the errors are getting bigger. In the past, my memories contained one small error; one or two. Nowadays they all contain one huge error. Between my memory and me there's this all-out wrestling match. And a gap that keeps getting bigger. Soon, if I grow old, I shall be saying things, when reminiscing, that have no connection whatsoever with anything I have read or learned. When I read "Marion goes to the ball," I will understand it as "Pierre works in the factory," which doesn't correspond to reality at all. I worry about these magnifications. What on earth is going on in the gap between what I have learned and what I say?

Above my bed (but off to the side, so that I can see it when I'm lying down) is a painting of an angel that I bought in Rome twenty years ago. Without realizing it, I had bought a very interesting painting (for 700 francs, which was a lot for me, since I was a student at the time), seventeenth-century if you please, depicting a baroque angel in court dress. Apparently—a scholarly friend told me this—it's a work from the

Bolivian Altiplano, a school of painting the epicenter of which was situated south of La Paz and which was noted not only for depicting angels armed with blunderbusses like conquistadors, but for always portraying them with cast shadows, "which is odd for disembodied creatures," as my friend pointed out.

My angel, like my fool, is peculiar. It's hard to tell, for example, where his arms begin. Often, in the evening, I look at him while thinking about something else and in my mind correct the outline so that the arms emerge at the right place. It's the same with the legs, which are oddly positioned (like THE FOOL's). As for the shadow, it always reminds me of the word *elytron*, which I have to look up in the dictionary, for there are certain words whose precise meaning obstinately refuses to lodge in my brain. Elytron means "the hard outer wing case of a coleopterous insect, which is not used for flying but covers and protects the hind wings in the manner of a sheath." Proof that I muddle everything: I associate elytra with butterflies. I used to think that, before turning into a butterfly, the poor, hapless insect had elytra and was forced to suffer this indignity. Not at all! I invent things, and it can be tiresome at times. It reminds me of a wonderful story by the Swiss writer Peter Bichsel, "Yodok," where a man starts using the same one word for everything: the word *yodok*. If he wants to say "that table is pretty," he says "that yodok is yodok." I love that story, it makes me laugh so hard it brings tears to my eyes.

I think that all writers would like to whittle things down to just one word. I also think that the most interesting writers of the last twenty, thirty or forty years are the German-speaking writers of Austria or Switzerland. If a writer is Austrian or Swiss, I read him. There's always a gap between him and his language. I also read him for the mountains. A writer without a mountain always leaves me with the impression that something is missing. The writer with a mountain doesn't go around botanizing all the time, but it's most unusual if, at some point or another, he doesn't go walking in his landscape.

It wasn't exactly in the mountains but in a fold in the hills that Mark met Cézanne one day. He had set out on the road to Le Tholonet to take photographs here and there, details of the landscape, for his private use. Perhaps it was hot—I no longer remember at what time of year he made the pilgrimage—no doubt he was carrying a little backpack—I don't know, I wasn't with him—but that his mind was full of Cézanne's work and thoughts, of that you can be sure. Then, lo and behold, slightly higher up on a path nearby, he saw a man approaching whom he immediately identified as a vagabond. The man's presence and gait made an odd impression, but he didn't really know why. They passed, and Mark made out the man's face clearly. It was only when he was back in Aix that he recognized him.

A vagabond isn't necessarily a revenant but there's definitely something of that kind about him. If he's a revenant it's because he has come back from the dead. THE FOOL walks in the grassy mountains in his cap and bells, holding the staff from which his bundle hangs at such a peculiar angle that you might mistake it for a flute, the flute with which he leads a whole town—of children, I believe—behind him. Orpheus did things like that.

I WASN'T PARTICULARLY FOND OF WALKING. It was the idea of walking I liked. And in a book, I always enjoyed the moment when the narrator or one of the characters sets off on a walk. On the condition that the walk was in the mountains or the woods, or, at a pinch, if all else failed, in the countryside; but in a town, no, never. A walk in a town is of no interest to me. I know what there is in a town, the things worth seeing in this or that establishment, this or that street or square: photography exists to point them out to us, not language.

I wasn't particularly fond of walking, but I knew quite a bit about the activity from novels and from my daydreams and desires. Then one day with Carl, because we needed to pass the time, and because, all things considered, the idea of a walk was the only thing that really appealed to us, we started walking in actual landscapes, and always, given the choice, in the mountains. With his knife, Carl would lop off hazel boughs and make walking sticks for us. At first, we would set out unprepared. Little by little, we got ourselves kitted out: a small backpack with a picnic, waterproof clothing and proper walking shoes.

At the point in the walk where I would have turned back, Carl always wanted to go a little further, a little higher, just a little, but steadily on. In the end, we would always go much further and much higher, and had someone said to me down in the valley: you'll be going all the way up there, I would have protested vigorously, refused and turned away.

It wasn't reaching the summit that I liked—views and panoramas leave me cold—it was the act of walking. Carl had a knack, so that, at one stage or another, every time, on every walk we undertook, we would stray from our appointed path for an hour or two. At first, this worried me. Being a city dweller, I was afraid we'd lose our way. Then, little by little, it became the high point of the walk: the moment when we were so completely lost in the mountain expanse that we had to abandon any idea of a past existence or turning back and were forced to venture forth and make our way through unknown defiles. On my own, I could never have managed this.

From time to time, I would observe Carl with his staff and bundle out of the corner of my eye. I would see him making his way over tufts of grass and stones in a desolate landscape that we didn't understand. Then one day, a good ten years or so after my friend Michel had given me the tarot pack, we were making our way along a sunken footpath under the trees when I saw that I was walking with THE FOOL and realized that THE FOOL was not only Orpheus or the Pied Piper of Hamelin, not only a revenant or a vagabond, but was also love. And that love, perhaps, was all of these things rolled into one.

Yet when I think of THE FOOL it's a vagabond I think of, a quite terrifying vagabond whom I myself must have met one day in the distant past; and that meeting on the wasteland must have so affected me that I lost, not my powers of speech—on the contrary, I recovered them—but my memories. Everything that had happened up until that point vanished into thin air. I remember that I was very scared but, at the same time, knew straightaway that it was the meeting I had long been waiting for: I was prepared for it. Before that, without knowing it, I'd been bored.

It took place in the mountains; far from the world, that is, far from life in society, under conditions of the utmost solitude. When I saw him arriving, with his cap and bells moving through the bracken, and had taken stock of just how isolated I was, with no possibility whatsoever of turning back, I naturally put on my mental armor. Here he is, I said to myself, don't be too afraid. If you're destined to meet like this, it's because you're able to face him. Don't try to flee, you would miss the most important meeting in your life. Meanwhile, THE FOOL's cap was drawing nearer. Face him, I repeated to myself. You're about to find yourself in the presence of death: you have what's needed to confront him. Speak to this man as you'd speak to anyone, and for heaven's sake don't try to put on clever airs, don't slink off—in any case, he won't let you.

So he emerged from the undergrowth and I began to make out his face and attributes. Yes, I thought to myself, with a kind of melancholy horror, it's him all right, it's THE FOOL. You think such things appear only on playing cards; you couldn't be more wrong. In reality, they exist in life. You're scared but, at the same time, it's horribly exciting to find yourself faced with an event of this kind. At that moment, you cease to possess that survival instinct characteristic of all living organisms, it seems. You're ready for anything, even defeat. It's the great orgiastic battle, the sublime point of existence, the great moment of bliss, should you choose to look at it that way. The long-awaited event which many people—and I, too, had labored under that illusion—confuse with falling in love.

He appeared a few yards off, and as with the angel from the Bolivian Altiplano and the figure in the tarot arcana, there was clearly something not right about him, something almost impossible to describe. Something unthinkable, unnameable, in the figure's composition, an abnormality easy to sense but difficult to pin down.

A child can confront an apparition of this kind. Knowing that, I became a child again. The moment I did this I found a way—someone must have shown it to me in the past, I imagine—I began telling a story at such high speed that it came as a surprise even to me. There was nothing he could do since I was speaking, and the story I was telling was quite good, it hung together nicely, unlike THE FOOL, who did not hang together nicely and, if anything, was falling apart. I managed to create a real landscape, the elements came easily, slotting neatly into place, I even managed to introduce a bit of color, there was no end to it and I didn't feel tired. Time, of course, as in any experience of this kind, had stopped. A different form of time came about, which in homage, ever since, I always write with a capital T. This particular form of Time — I understood this many years later — is the one found in narrative.

At this point, it's not a wall I come up against but a void: I have no idea what became of THE FOOL during our discussion — a discussion in which I did all the talking but which he responded to in a way. Sometimes I think I breathed new life into him and that, having started out as a dead figure, he went off alive, with his arms and legs henceforth in the right places, and his animal the identifiable kind, with its own unique coloring. Sometimes I think he vanished and, having rid myself of the Mistigri on the road to Yonville, I was able to return home, have pleasant little affairs, watch Berthe growing up and live a splendid life.

THE FOOL ISN'T ONLY THIS LAST, HOWEVER, since he's also the walking companion, love. When Carl appeared to me disguised as THE FOOL, we were making our way along a sunken footpath under the leaves. Moving below us to our left was a very clear stream where trout were darting about. Carl pointed out the trout to me, which I hadn't noticed. During our hikes, he often points out fish or birds to me. I never see them. Somehow I just can't disentangle the landscape. When he patiently persists in showing me a bird I can't see in the distance, like a pupil who doesn't dare tell his teacher again that he hasn't understood the explanation (if he's valiant and upright he will ask him twice, but the third time will give up, knowing that the teacher will lose patience), I eventually cry out—Oh yes! There it is! I can see the kestrel now! Fortunately, it's often just at that moment that the bird flies up.

I also go walking with Carl, then, so that he can point things out to me which I can't see. It's as if I were blind and THE FOOL had eyes. THE FOOL describes the landscape to me and I listen in order to learn. Thanks to THE FOOL I possess an additional set of bearings with which to find my way about in life: without him, I'd have to fumble around in a world where everything is so thoroughly tangled that all I can make out is this one puzzling image, not the component parts of that image, each in its proper order and place.

This particular fool is not in the least bit hostile or frightening. On the contrary, it's the one I have made a pact with. Is this perhaps what happened at the moment of the great meeting on the mountain? Is it this I know nothing of and am condemned to surmise? I didn't breathe new life into him to make him go away. He didn't vanish. I made a pact with him. To make a pact with the thing that threatens you is arguably the smartest trick of all.

What's no laughing matter, of course, is the cap and bells. Lepers used to have bells which they would ring on their approach to warn those in good health that they should stand aside or flee. Sometimes, to muffle the tinkling, I wrap the bells in my hands, an exercise that requires a certain contortion of the limbs. THE FOOL, then, is also myself, and whenever I see this wretched playing card, this pitiful cardboard rectangle with its crudely drawn and colored figure at the foot of my desk lamp, I tell myself that one day I must extend my range, spread my wings a little, for to be reduced to so wretched a figure is a little sad perhaps.

I'd like the frame to be bigger, and to no longer be frozen in the position of a revenant–vagabond–piper by this small strip of cardboard. Sometimes I take my angel from the Altiplano down and turn him face to another wall in a room I use for storage. I put my playing card away in a drawer. But what I then encounter is a void, not a space. If I go traveling to take my mind off things—and I've done a lot of traveling—I get bored without my fool. Something that exists only in my own home tugs at me, calling me back, and eight days later I'm home again. They say people who have been held hostage experience this: if they yield to their emotions, they want to go back into the trap, with its alternation of evil and healing powers. It's this back and forth that fascinates, this whirling round and round. It's this that sends you into raptures, mingling fear and ecstasy, ecstasy and fear.

There are all kinds of magic tricks you can perform to keep something threatening at bay. Children ought to be taught these things in school, like music and math. If, for example, I choose to focus on THE FOOL's luxuriant, springlike, cheerful aspect, how charming and good-natured this piper becomes! He's a good little companion who initiates you in the sciences of nature and painting and walks merrily at your side, playing pure and sprightly airs. He's a one-man spring. First magic trick: turn your other into spring.

If, on one of these happy hikes, as is bound to happen, at a turn in the path or in the glance of an eye, your other should all of a sudden reveal his awe-inspiring side, that face without a past which is tantamount to a death sentence, you have only to believe and to go on believing. To believe despite all the evidence to the contrary, to believe without requiring the tiniest scrap of proof, nourishing your belief on your own vitality, your own spring. At which point THE FOOL's face and gait become luxuriant once more, gentle in the sense that a person in the Middle Ages was said to be gentle—noble and cheerful, that is. Second magic trick: remain vigilant and attentive throughout. Work tirelessly to furnish spring.

Emma Bovary didn't know how to do this, no one had taught her how to do it, and it certainly wasn't at Tostes that she would have learned. THE FOOL appears to her not only as the blind man on the road to Yonville, he also comes into her own home in the guise of Lheureux, the evil hawker with a name so outrageous that even with no education and no prior warning she ought to have been on her guard. Madame Homais, for example, would have been on her guard. But Emma is so tempted by the trap, so tempted by death, that barely has she made out his figure than she's rushing out to greet him, and preferably in her finest dress.

IN A BOOK, THERE'S ALWAYS A WORD MISS-
ing. And the better and more finished the book, the
sharper the outline of the missing word, so much so
that we, the reader, can almost pronounce it. Once
the book has been published, the absence of that
word has a powerful knock-on effect on the author.
For months he tosses and turns in his sleep. He wants
to find that word he can't find. But his life, over time,
has become ever more closely bound up with his
books. So much so that he always finds the missing
word, not in the act of writing but in life. Overjoyed
at having found it, he starts writing a new book where
once again a word will be missing, and so on.

I think fondly of the missing word in *The Magic
Mountain*. The fondness I feel for *The Magic Mountain* comes not from *The Magic Mountain* itself but

from the word those six hundred or eight hundred pages try so desperately to find, and almost do find—how close we come!—when that utterly abnormal scene occurs: Hans Castorp hears a farmer in the mountains saying to someone, "Good day to you," and it changes his life.

How so? When you hear a perfectly ordinary phrase of that kind, your life isn't changed. But Hans Castorp, who so wants to die, just as Emma Bovary wants to die, has an ear that pricks up on hearing that tiny phrase, so happy and full of life, the phrase of a man who hasn't the slightest wish to depart this life, on the contrary, aspires to endure and maintain sociable, even friendly, ties with his fellow men. The phrase goes to his head. It won't be enough to save him, but thanks to that phrase he'll be able to survive a little longer and love Clavdia Chauchat. The missing word may be the one that enables you to go on living.

Because writers want to die. It's a family secret. People think they want fame; writers think that, too, but what they actually want is to be carried off as a small child in the arms of their father on that marvelous horse making its way through a German forest. "Who rides by the night in the wind so wild? / It is the father, with his child." *"Mein Sohn, was birgst du so bang dein Gesicht? / Siehst, Vater, du den Erlkönig nicht?/Den Erlenkönig mit Kron' und Schweif?/Mein Sohn, es ist ein Nebelstreif."* ("My son, what is it, why cover your face?/Father, you see him, there in that place/The elfin king with his cloak and crown?/It is only the mist rising up, my son.")

But it isn't only the mist, of course. It's death. Fathers can't see this. Only children can. Goethe was thirty-three when he wrote that poem. In the portrait painted by Joseph Karl Stieler in 1828, his face is magnificent. The look in his eyes (he was nearly eighty at the time) as he glances up at the Elfin King is at once skeptical and utterly transfixed, enchanted. No poem is quite so bloodcurdling: *"Mein Vater, mein Vater, jetzt fasst er mich an!/ Erlkönig hat mir ein Leids getan!"* ("Father, his fingers grip me, O,/The elfin king has hurt me so!"). The last line is full of pathos: "Locked in his arms, the child was dead." Meeting THE FOOL generates this kind of event. But perhaps you have to have died to become a writer?

There was a word missing from my previous book. For a long time I was tormented by this, then one day I found it as I was walking with Carl on a sunken footpath under the trees while moving along below us was a very clear stream where trout were darting about which I couldn't see. The word when it appeared came as a huge relief. I didn't even have to take advantage of it straightaway, I could keep my discovery secret the way you do when you have found a piece of treasure. At times like this, I'm particularly cheerful and relaxed, and nobody understands why, especially as they are periods when nothing remotely out of the ordinary seems to be happening in my life. But I knew I had the germ of my next book: I could sleep peacefully.

Recognizing THE FOOL in the man I loved gave me quite a start. There comes a moment—at first, it's not like that at all—when life and literature are so closely intertwined that it's almost as though you possessed magic powers and could conjure up in your existence things that happen in your books. This man you love suddenly becomes a man in your book. You even managed to fit *him* in. If you're a bit fearful, as I am much of the time, you try to keep the two worlds separate. No, no, you beseech I don't know whom, I don't want *him* mixed up in the landscape as well! I want him to stay behind in life! I want him as a counterpart to these (to my mind) bizarre and fascinating constructions. But it's not to be. He comes into the book. And, to make matters worse, he wants to. If he has loved you it's because he was there already or else wanted madly to come in.

I look at Carl who has chosen to come into my book, and I'm at once skeptical and enchanted. I can't help thinking that it's a bit odd to want to be in a book and that, for once, it's a desire I'm not familiar with. I question him about this in the act of love. Do you really want to be inside my book? Yes, yes, his body and feelings cry out in reply. He wants to be in my book, not so that he can be a character there but so that he can take part in it and live that form of life: being on the outside doesn't interest him at all. At times I can't help asking myself what mother could have fabricated such a son. And what father.

THE FOOL wants to come into a book, he wants to be part of the book, but sometimes—since the moment he looks round I discover yet another new aspect of his person—he sneaks in not as the man I love, not as a vagabond, not even as a revenant, but in court dress like my angel from the Altiplano. Just the other day, for example, Jean-Benoît came into my book clad in his lecturer's outfit. It was shortly before a meeting with his students, we were talking about those writers who pretend to be modest while secretly gnawing on the bone of ambition. In the same conversation we talked about Jean-Benoît's mother, who's eighty-eight, *Diloy le chemineau*, the question of houses to be sold or bought when your parents are dying, and how it feels to be in the bedroom you grew up in as a child. While we were chatting away very intensely, as we always do when we're together, I was also looking very intensely at his apartment, which I had never visited before. And it wasn't so much with my eyes, which were focused on my interlocutor, that I was doing this, but with my back and limbs, the nape of my neck. Jean-Benoît knew this. In two hours, I took in not only all of his books, the power of all the books brought together in his apartment, but also each of his carefully chosen objects, nearly all of which were linked to his childhood. I took in the two huge-trunked pine trees facing his balcony, the naked gardens, the missing squirrel, his distant past in this apartment and his more recent past. What friend will let you do this other than the friend who's already in your book? Then we went to meet his students, and as we always have lively conversations, he and I, the meeting went off well, the students were delighted. After that, we dined in a restaurant with A. and G. The charm might have worn off at this point, had Jean-Benoît not mentioned, for my benefit, an episode from his childhood. But the precise moment he came into my book—with his Altiplano costume, his elytra, his shadow, his cap and bells, and his staff where a flute might have been— was on the telephone the next day when he made a very brief remark about a murder. I had told him I was writing THE FOOL: he came in so that he could carry on living.

At this point you will say: but who or what exactly is THE FOOL? He's protean, forever changing shape and appearance, and has a variety of functions. I'm afraid so. If things were simple, we would know about it. If terror, love, friendship, death and madness referred to the same figure each time, we would know about that, too, and they would be less of a burden to us. What's marvelous is to be able to approach this protean, unsettling body, these sudden transformations of countenance and purpose, without getting so badly burned that you lose your powers of speech (the worst loss of all). If you can carry on living and find the words needed to look THE FOOL in the face, it means you're a writer, hanging there, protected. To be stronger than him is the only way to survive.

I'M GOING TO GO BACK TO THE BEGINNING. I'm all for doing things conscientiously, keeping a cool head. And besides, I like going back to the beginning: it brings me a kind of peace, a feeling of pleasure, like being curled up between the sheets of your bed in a quiet, warm apartment. THE FOOL, then. It's a nice word, with its inexplicable little dot in French. THE FOOL on my playing card at the foot of my desk lamp since I finished writing my last book, and was missing a word in that book, and found it as I was making my way along a path with Carl, et cetera.

That's how writers advance. Jean-Benoît's students asked very interesting questions. They were students from Orléans, a town where I was so unhappy. I lived there between the ages of eleven and seventeen. The town was gray, the sky was gray, everything was gray and ice-cold. Fortunately, I had a blue moped that saved my life. On my moped I would go speeding through the gray fields, under the gray sky, among the apple trees. To my mind, there was only one pretty thing around Orléans: the trees in blossom, there were lots of trees in blossom in spring. The trees in blossom and the moped saved my life. I was horribly unhappy at the time. I was in thrall to THE FOOL in his most baneful incarnation. THE FOOL held sway over my poor little life as a frail young girl, he was extremely powerful, he made me want to throw up and die. So, to get some air, I would climb onto my blue moped—a Peugeot 120—and go speeding off into the December cold, traveling twenty, thirty, forty kilometers, with sheets of newspaper stuffed under my pullover—my grandmother had taught me this as a way of protecting yourself against the cold. Sometimes I would deliberately go into a skid. Sometimes I would deliberately injure myself on the gravel and kill myself on the embankment.

The little apples were pretty. The region around Orléans, thank heavens, is a region of market gardens and orchards. Without that springtime, I would have died. THE FOOL wanted me dead and I responded to that desire, which was much more powerful than I, by a tactic I have adopted successfully ever since:

impeccability. I was an excellent pupil, I did my homework scrupulously. There were other pupils more gifted than I, but I had a constancy and earnestness that ensured I always got very good grades. Faced with THE FOOL: behave impeccably. That way, he can't touch you, he can't exert that destructive influence over you, he jumps about with all the attributes of a pernicious, murderous fool, he tries in vain to kill you. You're impeccable, things wash over you like water off a duck's back, you go about your life on your moped, you twist the gray throttle, and away it goes. How good it is to escape!

And that's how I became a writer. Because of THE FOOL and the tactics I employed to escape his clutches. It wasn't much fun. It took me a long time, in fact — really, a very long time — to escape his destructive, murderous clutches. Twenty years on, it makes my head swim when I think of the childlike ruses I adopted to pull the wool over his eyes. First it was the moped, then later — ten years later — the car. Apart from writing a story, there's nothing I like better than driving a car, alone. Each time, I escape — even if I'm only going round the corner — each time, I live through spring, the apple trees in blossom, I'm born again, I come back to life. Every summer, driving a car is my salvation.

I know other children who have found themselves in thrall to THE FOOL: little Miles and young Flora in *The Turn of the Screw*. I also know children who have never had that experience. Someone who has never crossed paths with THE FOOL, provided he has the necessary gifts, is destined for great things. For him, life rolls out its carpet without a shadow. It must be marvelous to advance in an endless summer where the obstacles melt away of their own accord. How happy one must feel to be alive! And so in step with the world that whenever you make a move, the world smiles back. You make another move? Again the response comes back: immediately, borne aloft on a silver platter. How easy it is, in that case, to become cheerful and good. If you mention THE FOOL to someone who has never met him, he listens politely as an expert in the art of happiness. He has never felt scared, but since he has always been happy he has become very intelligent, too: so he imagines THE FOOL, he sees exactly what you're talking about, he's informed about everything. For him, however, he's a figure on a playing card. He doesn't invest forms with life, since for him life is already present, complete in itself, with its accidents, no doubt, but nothing you can't skip over in a dignified fashion.

To go back to the beginning is to see him over and over again, rambling through the mountains in his fool's motley that separates him forever from the world of the living. Animals follow in his wake, uneasy but entranced. He's a figure from a fairy tale who performs miracles as he advances: the moment he happens by, everything is named. He happens by? The leaf he grazes with his shoulder shines brightly for an instant, named leaf all of a sudden, when prior to that it had been asleep in a dark mass of foliage. It's the same with grass or stones, his labors are at once unending, miraculous, and doomed to fail, for the moment he has happened by the things which have been named cease to be named, right behind his back.

He doesn't enjoy company, as we have seen. Anyone who spots him coming feels very uneasy; indeed, in a good many novels, and in life as well, we have seen families abruptly torn asunder, couples who loved each other hate each other, children in good health suddenly drop dead, horrific car crashes or worse in the vicinity of his ghastly, magisterial presence. He happens by and turmoil ensues. He happens by and you get one of those inexplicable moments, just when you were feeling happy and at peace with yourself, when everything clouds over, grows dark, comes crashing down. Even Virginia Woolf, who knew a great deal about the subject, went and threw herself in the Ouse when THE FOOL happened by. There are times, however, when you want to be carried off by him, you want to curl up in his icy chill, you want to gaze into his eyes which do so much harm and yet so much good. You're crazy when you're a writer.

UNLESS YOU HAVE HAD PARENTS, GRAND-
parents, and great-grandparents who were pioneers.
American writers, for example, have never had, and
never will have, a fool. That old antic moon has no
place in the New World. They stride on ahead without once looking back, fortified by having had parents, grandparents and great-grandparents who were
courageous individuals, intent on building. Whereas
we, who have done nothing but inherit, have so much
land to clear if we wish to build, that after rummag-
ing through all those ruins and coming across scraps
of treasure we're soon under a spell. If an American
writer sees a strange man, a vagabond, walking by,
he describes him in a healthy way, and he becomes
a character, perhaps even an unforgettable one. ("Ah
Bartleby! Ah humanity!") We, on the other hand,
live on so many tons of books, pictures and stories,

that fiction is our world. When we meet a man, he always belongs in a story, he's always in a painting.

To rid ourselves of THE FOOL, then, we'll have to reinvent history and the ancestors who brought us forth. To do this, like children who undress a doll to find out how it's made, we'll begin by removing his fool's cap, which is also the winged helmet of Mercury. Under that cap, what's his skull like? Hairy? Bald? How old is he? Next, we'll disentangle once and for all the bands of his bundle to see what's inside. A snack? The bundle is round and full: a ball? A globe? What for? Don't hesitate to ask him. It wouldn't be a bad idea either to throw out the bells; the man will at last stop tinkling as he walks and the conversation will be clearer, more audible. We'll question him about his eccentric way of placing over his right shoulder the staff he holds with his left hand. Why that position? Painful left shoulder? Tendonitis? Stiff neck? Just to show off, a way of drawing attention to yourself? We'll shoo away the dog, the beast with no color; or else we'll take him in, but on condition he states his identity, shape, and intentions. At this point, it's not impermissible—nothing is in this matter—to ask THE FOOL why all the other figures in the tarot are also him, in different guises. Last but by no means least, we'll ask him, very specifically, stressing each word, why he's the only figure in the arcana not to have a number. There we'll have him. Because the only creature in the world who can't be given a number is man.

The world has been under a spell for so long now that the spell needs to be broken if we're to advance a little. We may have to bid farewell to pleasure, to too much pleasure: become serious and valiant like an American pioneer; purchase a few acres of land, build a house on it and live there with our wife and children. I'm all for becoming a Puritan and singing hymns like William Blake and his wife, naked in the back of their garden. I'm all for abandoning, not music or books, for heaven's sake, nor all those pictures, but the fascination with which we look upon these things. I want to look at the world with a fresh eye, to be released from the spell that has held me captive since my birth, due to the circumstances of that birth. Being under a spell undoubtedly yields a good many poets, but it keeps you remote from the authentic man.

THE FOOL roams through the region of which Eudora Welty writes: "It took the mountain top, it seems to me now, to give me the sensation of independence. It was as if I'd discovered something I'd never tasted before in my short life." And THE FOOL really is on the mountain top, for though there are tufts of grass at his feet, on the horizon there's nothing. He must be right at the very top, therefore, higher than everything else. Henceforth you can meet him without feeling afraid, since you know that underneath his fool's cap he has a skull just like everyone else, and if his limbs are caught up in curious gymnastics, it's because his left shoulder hurts. Like a small child who's afraid of the wolves and ghosts that might be lurking in the attic, and has been led by the hand into that shadowy attic now filled with light, and been told: "There are no ghosts, you see. There aren't any wolves. They're just bits of old furniture, objects that have been stored here because they're of no use anymore," henceforth you can move freely on the mountain plateau of independent-mindedness, without being afraid you will meet some terrifying ghost from the past.

THE NARRATOR

A CHALET. A CHALET IN THE SNOW, AND A road leading up to it. The snow must have fallen last night and formed this dazzling white mantle, not a bird track anywhere, just the hint of a black hole here and there, a fence post in a field perhaps, perhaps a patch of earth. A car is making its way slowly up the road, which is itself blanketed in snow.

In the woods behind the chalet, animal eyes are gazing upon the scene from the gaps between trees. Since the color of an animal's fur corresponds to the seasons, you can't make out their shape or hue, but wherever you are, you can sense those bold eyes watching you. Nature is watching you. Hold on tight.

The moment the guilty man steps from the car, the following conviction is confirmed in him, shooting skyward like an arrow: it's the grass, the trees, the streams in particular, and even the keen, bracing air, that are the first to tell you how you should conduct yourself, why you are mistaken, in what ways you have sinned. As for the eyes of wild animals, they're the eyes of love, so it's not hard to understand their purpose, scattered throughout nature, while you in your wretched existence try to cheat in everything and on everyone. Look me in the eye, say the hind and roe, and you'll soon see if you're cheating or not.

Further back, the mountains begin, where in spring and summer it's a delight for all: the grasshoppers, the seated woman reading, the couple in shorts and hiking boots with a flask dangling from their knapsack. On the other side of the mountain is a town. We can disregard towns for the time being, since they belong in other people's books, and although we enjoy reading about them in other people's books, on our side of the mountain we have nothing to say about them. Town is, of course, where the narrator lives; it's where he tells the story, ensconced in his apartment. The rest of the time, however, he's on the road, roaming about, seeing wonderful or excruciating—and above all puzzling—things. Everything is incomprehensible when you first set eyes on it.

The narrator longs to go over to those animals with their bright, staring eyes, those vacant eyes glowing in the dark forest. Even so, he's relieved on his walks to find people in shorts and sunscreen traveling the roads. Oh, how he loves talking to them, how he loves being someone they can converse with! How wonderful to be welcomed among people who have no idea what he's doing out here, roaming on the edge of the forest! To hear them inquire in the evening, over supper in the dining room of the chalet: "Do you know the region well? How long will you be staying? What do you do for a living?" The narrator's so glad not to be viewed with suspicion, so glad to be seen as someone of sound morals and to be asked about his life as though it were a real, normal existence. He invents: Yes, he's on vacation. The question of his profession is a bit trickier, but he comes up with an answer. He even gets roped in at times: "Will you come walking with us tomorrow?" He accepts, of course. Who would be brazen enough to say: "What! Don't you know? I'm the narrator!"

So the next day he goes walking with them. He's friendly and considerate and full of high spirits, for he's eager to make a good impression, eager to gain acceptance for a moment and enjoy the fleeting sense the walk will give him of being with others. With Eva and Yvan, Véronique, Alain, and Patricia, he tries to walk at the same pace, laugh at the same things, take an interest in the same discoveries. He observes how they go about acting more or less alike. Gradually, confusedly, they begin to sense a difference. They couldn't put a name to it, but there's something about the narrator that unnerves them.

He can sense their mistrust; it saddens him, he would so love to be mistaken for one of them. Some of them overcome the awkward hurdle and suspect the narrator is a narrator, or someone peculiar at any rate, but even so they don't hold it against him. They don't pry into his secret. They sense there is one but feel they shouldn't intrude. Or else they simply have no wish to. Still, he finds these walks a bit tiresome, as he has to tread very carefully. He always comes back feeling sad because the true bonding has never occurred. But you're an outcast, poor narrator, and an outcast you will always be. Given how much you enjoy telling a story, put a brave face on your banishment. Some outcasts can't even tell a story.

Outcasts who can't even tell a story are what one might call dropouts, lunatics, misfits. With them the narrator feels on a firm footing, albeit with one huge advantage: he can tell a story. They don't hold this against him, which is strange. Why don't they hold it against him, when telling a story would set them free? Perhaps they have given up, worn out by the long years of suffering. Yet because they still carry the fiery tablet inside them, the one that throbs, the one that would like to tell a story for two hundred and fifty pages and would like it to be beautiful, they find in the narrator someone who can do this for them. *You*, they sense, will avenge us for a lifetime of humiliation and defeat; *you* will tell our collective story.

The narrator's proud to have this gift and proud that his friends encourage him to make use of it. Proud the way a child is proud when he says his father is a fireman. What's strange is that it's not with his friends that he feels a sense of guilt. It's with the others, and only with the others: the Evas and Yvans, the Alains, Véroniques, and Patricias, from whom he carefully conceals his banishment, whom he mimics in order to win their trust, and in whose company he tries to learn, if only for a moment, how to live a normal life.

II

SOMETIMES HE LOSES TRACK OF THEM IN the mountains and finds himself alone on a bare slope, cast out into the wilderness, which questions him haughtily: "What have you done for me today? How have you celebrated me? What! You haven't celebrated me? What on earth can you be thinking? Do you really imagine you have a thousand years to loaf around? Get to work! Get to work!" Nature is implacable. So he stands there all alone, with a few flowers he has picked wilting in his hand. Because most of the time he doesn't tell a story. He spends the better part of his life waiting for the power to return, desiring it more than anything—more than another human being, more than another body. For a month or two, he'll tell a story, then the walks will resume for a year, the power will return, and so on and so forth, if all goes well, until his ninetieth year, at which point you will die, narrator, just like everyone else.

That night, while the others were sleeping—Eva with Yvan, Alain with Véronique, Patricia alone in her room—he went outside, summoned by the cold and snow which reminded him of Christmas. The moment the door was closed, he breathed in the metallic air and gazed up at the moon shining in the dark blue sky. Outside the chalet, a streetlamp lit up the road for fifty yards or so, after which there was pitch darkness. He set off along the road, his hands in his overcoat pockets and a woolly hat pulled down over his head. After fifty yards, he stepped into the darkness and disappeared.

His heart was glutted, heavy with all the images he'd amassed. He shuffled them, then glanced through them like a deck of cards. Did he examine them in detail? Sometimes, but mostly it was just for the pleasure of manipulating them. And it was by playing this game—place this one here, cover it with that one, take up this other one—that he earned his living: a narrator must earn a living, otherwise he disappears. The others, asleep in the chalet, probably had no idea he engaged in such activities. Or did they? It comes as a surprise sometimes, in one's superciliousness, to discover that we all know the same things. It's one of the reasons the narrator is so drawn to people who lead normal lives and so keen to be welcomed into their midst for a spell.

That afternoon they had climbed a hill planted with boxwood, as though they might expect to find a castle at the top. Which is exactly what happened: at the top of the hill they came across a ruined castle. Patricia was spellbound, Yvan and Eva fell in love, Alain and Véronique held hands, the narrator tagged along at the back, glad of the company of these friends. Since Yvan knew a fair bit about French history, he had some interesting things to say about the castle and what had happened there. The narrator listened carefully, but didn't retain a thing. Yvan's words went straight in one ear and out the other. The narrator isn't interested in history, it's one of his many dozens of failings. He isn't interested in science either and can no more remember the names of stars than he can those of plants.

In the evening, his friends at the chalet sometimes discussed politics. Here, the narrator had to bow out from the very first words. He wasn't remotely interested in politics. At moments like this, the others were a little wary of him. What! A man of forty who was a teacher or a librarian—that was the profession he had given—but took no part in a discussion about politics? That was distinctly odd. They would scold him for this, especially Véronique, who knew a lot about politics and was up in arms about any number of things. He would stall, trying quickly to understand, then side with this or that speaker so as not to appear too apathetic.

They talk about politics, they know all sorts of things and the narrator is quite lost. It's at moments like this that he sometimes gets scared, wondering what right he has to be a narrator when he knows so little about the world. He listens and tries to learn, but doesn't remember a thing. The same instant he forgets. These things don't get etched in his brain. It's as though his brain can only remember bodies, mouths, facial expressions. "Part of my brain is dead," the narrator says to himself. "Another part is as ravenous as a mother or a bird of prey, snatching up anything that interests it." He manages to say that he has never voted—that people on the right give him the impression he's on the left, people on the left that he's on the right—but that he's certainly not an extremist. The narrator's a laughingstock when he's not telling a story.

III

NEVERTHELESS, HE'S BEGINNING TO ENJOY life at the chalet, so much so that he decides to spend not only the winter there, but the following summer, too. Lodgers of all sorts come and go, since the house, which is run by Madame Saintier, takes paying guests. And as it's pretty and nicely situated, people turn up all year round to spend a weekend or a week there.

The narrator has opted for the "red room"—the one with the cherry-red curtains and matching bedspread—and has arranged with Madame Saintier to pay a monthly rate from now on. She's a little alarmed by the length of his stay, and even more alarmed by the fact that he never receives mail or seems to phone anyone. "Might you be all alone in the world, Monsieur Real?" (it was the name he had given when signing in), she asks him with an awkward little laugh. He bridles at the suggestion and makes no reply. His unfailing old-world courtesy (a crucial attribute of narrators the world over) prevents Madame Saintier from inquiring further. Besides, he always pays on time, never makes a disturbance, and never invites anyone up to his room.

In his cherry-red room, the narrator reads a lot. Apart from telling a story, it's his favorite pastime. It's only natural: in the company of other narrators, he feels at home and finds a family and friends. It means a lot to him, since despite his peculiar station in life, the narrator has a heart, like everyone else. He has no appetite for complete solitude.

"Hmmm," he almost feels slightly aroused by Madame Saintier. And she's slightly aroused by him, too.

He's not bad-looking, and there's his solitude, which is particularly attractive to others because it seems so untroubled and, for that reason, enigmatic. When the narrator is out, little Madame Saintier goes up to his room and rummages about under the pretense of doing the dusting and tidying up. She notes the presence of a large number of books, but finds nothing in the way of papers since he takes his notebooks with him. "You'd think he was lying low," Madame Saintier confides to her husband one evening. "He's a strange fellow. What do you think of him?" Monsieur Saintier thinks nothing, only that his wife is troubled by this lodger, which troubles him, too, prompting him to make love to her rather more frequently than usual. "A shady character? A gangster? An ex-con?" wonders Madame Saintier as Monsieur Saintier pounds away at her. In this way, narrators give happiness wherever they may be. Their enigmatic presence boosts the erotic output of their entourage.

Lying in bed reading, the narrator hears the Saintiers' bed creaking. He smiles, puts down his book and listens closely. It's confirmation of his presence, proof that he exists. "I know who I am," he tells himself, "when the people around me make love." "I'm like a child, in other words, a baby at the breast. Yes, that's exactly it." Whereupon he falls happily asleep, after placing his hand almost absentmindedly on his crotch, just to be sure. And then he dreams, for he dreams a lot. In his dreams he has elaborate adventures which he thinks about when he wakes up the next morning. He dips into them and splashes about, dwelling on words that had come to him in the dream: "Doe," he muses, "she was speaking 'doe talk.'" And when Madame Saintier comes into the dining room where he's having breakfast, he already feels fired up by "doe talk" and all these words that have opened tunnels of greenery in his soul and are urging him out into the world, to live and rejoice, because he'll be seeking traces of them there. And "doe talk" will lead him on elsewhere, further afield, even if he remains in the chalet with Monsieur and Madame Saintier.

The narrator's cheerfulness amazes Madame Saintier, for she can see no grounds for it. Sometimes she puts it down to a sunny disposition—"It's very pleasant," she tells Monsieur Saintier, "he's always in good spirits"—and, at other times, to all kinds of horrific secrets: "What's he so cheerful about? It gets on your nerves after a while!" And by asking the narrator about his seclusion—he's been there for several weeks now and seems to have no plans or appointments in the region—she tries to upset him and make him unhappy, for above all she would like him to go to pieces; that way, she could comfort him and think he's just like all the rest.

The narrator, however, is no longer a boy of

twenty—he has never been a boy of twenty, in fact—and doesn't fall into these crudely laid traps. Over time, though, he has learned to act as if he had. Madame Saintier is so relieved when he seems willing to confide in her—a cry from the heart, a confession of failure! How her breast swells with pride! How bright-eyed and youthful she becomes! It's at this point that all Madame Saintier's pent-up affections come gushing out, her arms become smooth and vigorous once more, she, too, can start dancing and living again. "He's just like us! He's just like us," she thinks to herself, while merrily hanging out the wash in the garden. It fills her with longing: the longing to devour.

The narrator, meanwhile, has a pretty good idea how and when to feign a breakdown. It's never when he's genuinely at risk of one. At moments like that, never. It's a golden rule, to be set down in letters of fire: *never*. For were he to crack, he'd be struck dead by god-awful compassion. He just has to act up slightly, without overdoing it, as though held in check by a sense of propriety, when his opponent's belief in the imminence of his defeat has reached such a pitch that he would be abominated and cast out forevermore were he to remain unmoved. Only with his friends, the lunatics and misfits, can he reveal that, like a murderer, he never goes to pieces.

They find it rather agreeable, this fellow who's never a burden. And on days when he longs to die and lose his footing, his friends could not be more companionable: they die and lose their footing with him, to keep him company.

IV

MADAME SAINTIER HAS COOKED UP A STORY so that she can go walking with him in the mountains: the need for a stroll, a breath of fresh air, a view of the peaks. He can't decently refuse, so off they go together. Since she imagines he is some sort of intellectual, or interested in "spiritual matters" at any rate, she talks to him for half a mile or more about the books she's been reading. Much to her surprise, he has nothing very interesting to say. Maybe he's not so clever after all? He keeps up a steady barrage of questions, creating a diversion by asking her about the names of plants and rivers and villages, but she keeps coming back to the books she's been reading. She wants a straight answer, thinks the narrator, somewhat alarmed.

A great battle is being played out between them in the mountains. She says the most appalling things, such as: "I love poetry. And you Monsieur Real, do you like poetry?" Beads of sweat are forming on his brow. He can't bring himself to use the word "poetry"—not here, not with this woman. He ducks and weaves, cracks jokes. Not noticing she's tormenting him, but sensing it a little all the same, she pushes on. She wants to force him to confess; with her womanish wiles, she has understood exactly where his weakness and his terror lie. She wants to break in there, destroy this pseudomystery with the snap of a finger, and have this man with his superior airs see himself for what he is: a windbag and a prig.

She's very clever at this, or else he's particularly inept; either way, he's incapable of defending himself. At the end of his tether, he halts suddenly on the path, wheels round and, looking her straight in the face, blurts out: "For heaven's sake, stop!" "What is it?" she asks, feigning surprise. "Is something the matter? Did I say something to ..." For a full five minutes, marching briskly at her side, he'll say nothing further, not a word. Neither will she, a touch disconcerted but shrewd enough to know she has scored a hit. "You know," she tells Monsieur Saintier in the evening, as she removes her clothes to lie down at his side, "he's not as well read as all that. In fact, he's not really interested in anything much." "Hmmm ..." thinks Monsieur Saintier, "he rejected her and she's furious." And because Monsieur Saintier is kind, as so many men are kind to women with desires so insane that they're forever on the verge of losing their minds, he adds: "The walk, at any rate, did you the world of good. You look gorgeous." And so Madame Saintier feels reassured by the two great discoveries of the day: one, she's still desirable; and two, human beings are not so mysterious, after all.

V

IN THE CHERRY-RED ROOM, THE IMAGES came crowding in, slowly at first, as if holding hands. The narrator was surprised to see memories he attached no great importance to arriving—they were the only ones, in fact, to appear—in the form of a troupe of actors from the afterlife. Some were giving him signals that, though he didn't understand them, seemed familiar. They were making mischievous, euphoric, spiteful faces. It was as though, in the games they were playing, he risked being raped, or burned alive, or bewitched, and would derive unspeakable pleasure from this. "Please don't," he murmured. But the images were horribly enticing, for they were embodied in faces, landscapes, words. They went like a corkscrew through his soul. "I'm coming, I'm coming," gasped the narrator. He now found himself pinned to his bed like a moth before a lamp, beating his wings and stammering while the big dipper of space and time hurtled toward him. "No, no," he pleaded, like a woman who had been abducted, while in his parched body and soul everything cried out *yes* with such force that a cataclysm erupted outside. The chalet, Monsieur and Madame Saintier, the lodgers, the woods, the meadows, the fields, the towns—all came gently tumbling down until nothing remained of the world but the dreadful, intoxicating red room, where he was going to have to wrestle with the ghostly apparitions of dreams.

From time to time, he would go outside. Nothing remained. The narrator rubbed his hands with glee. A long way off, engulfed in dense fog, Madame Saintier continued to search for him so that they could talk about literature. On another side of the mountain, barely recognizable in the gloom, was a merry group clamoring for him to join them on a walk. Just to make sure, he went back up to his room. There was indeed a fire there, an enormous, stationary fire which wouldn't budge, refused to budge, until he had begun the story. He was alone in the world. He was overjoyed. He had always been alone in the world.

He acquainted himself with the forms. One of them was so desperate to gain his attention and had such beautiful gray eyes that he gently kissed her foot. Another was grotesque and drove him wild: he sodomized her on the spot, howling with energy and delight. The beasts had come out of the woods and were gathered round in a circle, staring into the red room with their gleaming eyes. The narrator could no longer see any difference between these beasts and his raptures among the ghostly forms that were inviting him to one thing only: an orgy.

Giving himself up to the task unreservedly, the narrator made love that night seventeen or twenty-seven times to bodies that were all different and all infatuated with murder. "The story! The story!" they pleaded, their wide-open mouths writhing with pleasure. "I have the story, I have the story," he reassured them between grunts. And when he had told the story well, they would all come at the same moment with great cries. "Tell me who I remind you of!" demanded a skinny little girl with pointed breasts. Toiling away at her, he replied: "You remind me of an emotion I once felt in London, when I was waiting for a woman who failed to show up." "Yes, that's me all right," said the young girl, shuddering under the blows. "Well spotted," she went on, hiccupping, "you're on the right track." "And me?" asked another, a big fat one, as she slipped deftly between the narrator and the young girl. He set to work on her, too. "You're that emotion I felt when I was twelve. I had to …" "Yeah, I know," replied the girl. "That's me all right, that's me …" By midnight, the narrator was quite worn out. "I want to go to sleep," he protested. "Are you leaving us?" asked the forms. "Yes, I'm exhausted," he replied, "so exhausted that I want to be far away from you for the night. But I'm so enamored of you all that I'd like to see you again in the morning."

Needless to say, the longer this life went on—for it's not often that forms turn up in a troupe like this and cause so much joy, only to vanish into thin air, though it does occasionally happen—the more impeccably the narrator behaved. He became a perfect little saint, insufferable, always merry, always friendly, always polite. So much so that Madame Saintier— offended, outraged by the insulting character over- obligingness can sometimes have, because of the profound indifference it displays—would throw up her arms in exasperation: "What a toady," she would say to her husband, abandoning any pretense at distinction. Then, with a haughty air: "I hate this incessant fawning on others. I think he's a bit obsequious, you know."

But for the narrator—as for those serial killers who, much to everyone's surprise, turn out to have been good husbands, good fathers, good friends—it was a question of protecting behind indestructible walls the rites being acted out in his secret room. And since the highest and thickest of these is the wall formed by impeccable conduct, like so many others before him and in the world around him, he built it, with a little inward smile, a little thrill at the thought of presenting to the world a facade so smooth that nobody could find a point of entry as they wore themselves out looking for the chink in the armor. "He can't be that nice," thought Madame Saintier. "He must be hiding something. Perhaps he's a bit kinky?" Then, lying down next to Monsieur Saintier: "I think he's in love with me." And shrewdly, much more shrewdly than the great clock he always came across as, Monsieur Saintier replied: "Why not? You're eminently desirable, my love."

VI

BUT THE NARRATOR ISN'T ALWAYS SUCH A fine fellow. If he's delighted to be a riddle to the likes of Madame Saintier, it's not simply because it allows him to sit quietly on his own with his imaginings, but above all perhaps because it gives him an exhilarating sense of superiority. To feel holier-than-thou with your precious images, yes, yes, that's all very fine. But to feel smug simply because you're alone, simply because you're different from others and in possession of a secret—morally, that's not so good. The narrator, who's ever so friendly and polite, who gets so much pleasure from misleading people, from appearing more foolish than he is, and from being mistaken for someone else, because of the power it allows him to wield, runs into a problem when he has to deal with someone less ingenuous than Madame Saintier. Then danger lurks.

If he's with Brigitte, for example, who makes films, or Valentin, who writes novels, or Olivier, who dabbles in conceptual art, the narrator feels a hundred times less comfortable than in the company of his backpacking friends at the chalet. For the terrible thing about the Brigittes and Valentins and Oliviers is that they think the narrator is just the same as them. At this point, the great show of invisibility he had put on for the ingenuous—who can be cruel at times, of course, but are so easy to dominate—is of no use whatsoever. What can he do to stay on top of things? For when the narrator's no longer on top of things, he's lost. Yet people like Brigitte, Valentin, and Olivier, who think he's no different from them (god forbid!), are all but impervious to his authority. What other strategy can he adopt? What can he do to be an object of speculation and conjecture to them, to be desired and feared by them? The poor narrator's in a sweat and looks truly pathetic.

Still worse—for he can handle the occasional defeat—is when the ingenuous and the Brigitte–Valentin–Oliviers come together. In that case, the ingenuous will witness his defeat for themselves. They who were awaiting one thing only—his breakdown—yet were fearful in his presence and plagued by doubts; who found him annoying, yet were bound to him by the riddle of his identity: with a huge sigh of relief, they side at once with those who slay the narrator by considering him no different from themselves. The thrill this gives them (the ingenuous) is enormous. At last they have the final say.

Fortunately, in the ingenuous camp there's nearly always an unsullied soul who will step up to try and save the narrator. Someone who senses his panic and suffering; someone who's never thought of dominating others and is none the worse off for it; someone who will compliment him and sing his praises from the rooftops. The narrator is so relieved—the other has saved him—and so grateful, that he will even consider laying down his life for his savior. So great is the love he feels for him (or her) that he's ready to drop everything, to abandon his stories and his complicated games on the spot. Not that the other had asked for anything in return. He was just being kind because he sensed the narrator's distress and because it's in his nature to aid people in distress.

In the presence of these ideal mothers, the narrator concedes defeat. Love me, he demands. Say I'm the most handsome, the most gifted, the most feared, the most desirable. Exaggerate my importance. The other doesn't go quite that far, he's much more subtle than the narrator, and not in a calculating way, but by nature. The other, who has never had a bone to pick with language and, mysteriously, has no wish to finish anyone off, does something unheard-of: he restores the narrator's dignity without setting him apart from others. And it is here, the one truly indestructible place that the narrator has always longed to be. It's the place he's obscurely seeking when he tries to bond with the fools, who aren't so foolish after all. It might even be, he thinks to himself, swept along by his boundless gratitude (it was a close shave), the place that will allow him to tell a sensible story at last, something truly beautiful and moving. And turning to his new friend, he declares: "The real narrator, the ideal narrator, is you." "Me?" asks the other, glancing at him with a wry smile. "Me? I have no imagination!"

With his new friend the narrator goes walking in the mountains. He tells him everything—his fears, his strategies for avoiding a breakdown, his hopes and desires. The other listens in silence and, every now and then, asks a question. Never once does he fall into the trap laid for him by the narrator's eloquence. For the narrator, to see someone good-natured and affectionate avoiding the trap he has laid comes as a huge relief. However, isn't this still a form of dominance? Is he not taking advantage of this gentle soul? Suppose his new friend were to suffer: would the narrator be responsive to his pain? Isn't it just another of those tricks he deserves to be hanged for?

No, there's no getting round the fact, he's only really at home with lunatics. That's probably why he spends so much time in prisons and mental wards, if only as a visitor. Nothing could be more suspect, for example, than the exhilaration he feels when he goes to visit his friend Fanny, who lives, I'm sorry to say, in what can only be called a mental asylum. How he mistrusts all those fine, noble feelings that spring to their feet, jostling for attention—Me! Me!, they all cry, Me first!—the moment he boards the train that will take him to Fanny. Even the word *asylum* appeals to him. If he were sane, instead of spending the day there with his friend, his ears taut as drumskins, he would blow his top, get her out of there, rant and rave, shower her with blows so that she'd make up her mind on the spot to return to the land of the living. But he doesn't. He's all eyes and ears. He's measuring himself against a story told by a young girl whom Fanny has introduced him to, who's convinced she has murdered her parents and, much to her astonishment, comes across mounds of corpses in the woods. Or against this other patient who's saying the kind of things people say in dreams. How well he understands them (he believes)! How easy it is to bond with them! Here, at least, he can be sure nobody is threatening him. He struts about like a peacock at the center of a defenseless horde.

Narrator, it's not good to behave in this way. Were you at all serious, you would love your fellow men and go among them without being afraid they will attack you, without wanting to mesmerize them in order to render them harmless. Go on, take a closer look: is there anyone you sleep next to at night without worrying they will murder you? Anyone in whose presence you are neither visible nor invisible but like a person alone with his dreams and recollections? "I don't know . . . ," says the narrator. Well then, search. A few fleeting images flit through him: "No, I can't see anyone . . . ," he repeats. Go on, I insist. The narrator's heart starts pounding. Faster and faster. He thinks of a name. He can't put a name to the name. It's the name that would explain everything.

VII

WHAT KIND OF MOTHER, THEN, GAVE BIRTH to the narrator? He recalls an elusive, very tall woman who paid very little attention to him. From time to time, as though at the end of her tether, she would stride off into the mountains, scattering on her path small herds of quietly grazing goats, and sending up in what can only have been her fury—her utter fury— flights of birds bursting out of the foliage. The very stones on the paths would come bounding, hurtling downhill as she tramped through the dust like Atalanta. Standing dumbfounded at the foot of the path, the tiny infant narrator feels the stones ricocheting off his ankles as they come tumbling down behind his fleeing mother. "Maman!" he probably cries out. But she doesn't look round; she's so far away now that she can't hear a thing. "Maman!" he shouts at the top of his lungs. And the young nanny goats come down to give him succor and support. He's three years old, sturdy on his legs already, and his heart is stubborn: surrounded by the goats, imprisoned in their foam, he sets out to climb the hill, a hundred yards or so behind the furious or despairing long legs of his mother plowing their way up the path.

And in this way, he grows. On the path behind his fleeing mother, who is quite mad and quite determined — determined perhaps to fling herself from the top of the hill onto the rocks that tumble down the other slope — he's five now, then seven, then twelve, then twenty. The goats get smaller. He himself is as tall as the giant Antaeus. All of a sudden, he towers over everything: the hill, the landscape, the region. He can still see his mother with her beautiful brown legs, her long legs running to fling themselves where exactly? Onto the rocks? He must stop her. He must get there in time to prevent her from flinging herself onto the rocks and dashing her pretty body, her motherly heart and mind, to pieces. How the little three-year-old narrator runs! It's because he's running behind his mother to prevent her from dying that he's a narrator. And as he runs, much to his surprise he's overcome with joy. It's his first experience of joy. He has all the scents of the wild thyme underfoot, the stench of sweat from the goats clambering up the hill all round him, the sensation of heat and the stones bouncing off his ankles, the knowledge of the force that has taken hold of him since he was turned into a giant by running behind her.

And then she disappears. She has vanished into thin air. He inspects the rocks: she isn't there. Her great magisterial body isn't there. He rummages in the undergrowth: she isn't there. He climbs onto the highest hill to get a good look at the landscape: nowhere is her great mouth at rest, nowhere can her huge body be seen, her long legs are missing. Very well, decides the narrator: you will turn into a landscape. And so, on the top of the hill where she has vanished forever, he decides that his mother has turned into a landscape and is now in the grass and flowers, the woods and fields. When he walks there forever, how can he fail to be happy and in his element, his absolute element?

What the narrator would like is to lie down in the flowers, smile at the passing sky, sing a little song in which the same syllable is repeated over and over, lose himself in the giddying repetitions and then feel the earth yawn open and swallow him up. And then start afresh. Lie down in the same meadow ten yards further on, sing his little song, repeat the same syllable over and over, and feel the earth yawn open and swallow him up, and then start afresh. Lie down ten yards further on, work himself into a frenzy singing quietly to himself, laugh at the thrill of feeling himself snatched away, swallowed up and devoured. And then start afresh. Needless to say, he can't indulge in these intimate little orgies when Madame Saintier is around. He has to be alone. But when he returns to the chalet, his back covered with scratches from rubbing against all that dry grass, and a bit spooked by all that humming and smiling to himself, how glad he is to find everything exactly as he had left it, with the wash hung out in the garden and his hostess looking stern or flinty or with a little smirk on her face. What the narrator likes is being left to his own devices, and then discovering, when he gets back, that nothing has changed.

VIII

MADAME SAINTIER HAS MELLOWED. THE narrator is a lot less scared of her, though he's still on his guard; and she's hardly afraid of him at all anymore, she's beginning to understand him. Very gently, as if butter wouldn't melt in his mouth, and laughing copiously to hide his embarrassment, he has begun talking to her about poetry, jumping back with a shout whenever he has grazed the enchanted circle. And now that she has understood how important it is at times like this to keep a cool head and show him a little extra affection—just a tiny bit more, barely perceptible—she plays the part of midwife almost to perfection. Here he is, waving his arms about like a madman, in her presence he's no longer afraid of approaching the circle at the risk of getting burned: she stands there without flinching, like a schoolmistress. The good she does him! "You know," he tells her, now that they are on more intimate terms, "I think I have a knack for turning the people I love into midwives."

She laughs, because she laughs now. Henceforth, she understands humor, jest, irony, the perverse streak peculiar to narrators and their inviolate childhood. Sometimes he takes her by the hand and prances about like a feebleminded child. She doesn't bat an eye, but prances about with him. They can be seen passing along the ridge, prancing about like figures in a shadow play: she in her tailored suit or in one of those outfits that are a little too showy for a walk in the mountains; he, the invisible one, growing visible now thanks to her. Monsieur Saintier, who is positioned behind a window in the chalet, observing the scene through binoculars, is dumbfounded and slightly aroused by it all: "She's crazy!" he thinks fondly. He'd always known she was crazy, it's what he likes about her. She's crazy and at the same time serious; in other words, she's beginning to love. She has understood that, in order to love the narrator, she must merge with his shadow, accompany and support him, dance a jig with him — and then withdraw when he seems utterly indifferent all of a sudden. Is he interested in my body? she wonders. He is, since he pounces on her from time to time and appears to be mad about her breasts, her thighs, her entire anatomy. Then suddenly he pulls away and seems to lose all interest in her body. "Let's wait and see," Madame Saintier says to herself, "there's something odd going on."

IX

WHEN THE NARRATOR HOLDS NOT THE slightest attraction for anyone, he wanders through cities and landscapes as if he didn't exist, as if he were the memory of himself. He barely inhabits the hotels he stays in, barely ruffles the sheets he sleeps between. Were you to take a photo of a bus he was on, he might not appear in it. In his place, you'd see an empty seat.

When he's in this state and roaming about the countryside, he's identical in every respect to the tarot card for death. He's also the most solitary of creatures, since death is the one figure in the world not to have a companion. Joy walks with sorrow, wisdom with folly, Sancho Panza with Don Quixote, Ophelia with Hamlet, Hector with Achilles; death, however, always walks alone. She has no companion to reign over and none to reign over her. Her one redeeming feature is that she's practically invisible, except to little children. Only they, who so love being made to laugh, only they see her as I see you—approaching, entering, quietly biding her time. Only they can perhaps convince her to relinquish her plans. They speak her language, the language of death being different from the language of the living. Little children speak that language up to the age of six or seven, at which point they grow feebleminded and well-adjusted for the most part, and remain that way until the age of twelve or so, when they begin to suffer. Their sufferings are put down to the transformation of their bodies, the difficulties they encounter coming ashore on the continent of sex. In reality, a twelve-year-old child suffers from the amnesia that has taken hold of him. He used to speak the language, he knew how to deal with death, he could see her, she wasn't especially frightening, he was big enough to confront her. Then, all of a sudden, the language he once spoke has been forgotten. Now he has zero power over death. Isn't losing that power the same as losing one's life?

And if, at times, the narrator so enjoys the company of babies, so enjoys bonding with them while their mothers keep a wary eye on him, sensing that what's flowing between them is not quite kosher, it's because there are times when nobody else can understand him. Just as when he's in the presence of a second narrator and, unbeknownst to others, they exchange one of those smiles or glances that mean: "I know who you are. I speak your language," so, between babies and the narrator, a private conversation washes back and forth, fluid and dark, which the baby gorges on like a love potion or a slug of gin. In the narrator's presence, babies fall into a sort of goggle-eyed trance, babbling the same sounds over and over, the ones that open onto the underworld where the darling bodies that have lived, loved, suffered and desired now reside and cry out for a story.

X

IN THE COUNTRY ASYLUM WHERE FANNY lives, a man has committed suicide, a friend of hers. He's thrown himself under a train "to ensure nobody will be able to identify him," says Fanny. The narrator, who has come to visit his friend, listens and shares in her grief. They're each seated in an armchair, and between them is this hole, this whirling void, this man she saw at breakfast yesterday who, rather than hang himself, say, has thrown himself under a train, "to ensure nobody will be able to identify him."

The narrator, needless to say, is at a loss for words. There are no words to express this thing directly. Words circle overhead, trying to draw a line around this poor, mangled body, this poor spirit — God rest his soul — crushed by the machine. "I'd like there to be a Mass," says Fanny, "a celebration. I'll see if I can arrange for one to be said. I'm not religious, but a mass would do us all some good." She's reached the stage where she's burying her dead, thinks the narrator to himself. There's progress for you! That's what I call success!

They spend three days together, and all the while, lying between them, guarded by them, watched over by them, is the body of this poor man crushed by the machine. Both are pious, both are bent in prayer over the mutilated body, while the world welcomes in triumph someone or other whose evil wishes have been crowned with success. We live in a century that bows down before cruelty, muses the narrator. It shapes the Fannys and the suicides, the friends at the chateau battling to safeguard their dignity. Oh, I shall avenge you, I'm determined to avenge you, thinks the furious narrator. I would much rather be here with you than among those apes besotted with power who carry all the envious blockheads and nonentities in their wake. "But, alas, we don't like fighting, and that's where we fall down," he confides to his friend. "We like to ramble around, experiencing all kinds of keen, delicate emotions; but more than anything, we feel as a delight, an inexpressible blessing, the gift bestowed on us of being able to converse with death on equal terms, walking in the mountains among the succulent grasses. We have such stupendous conversations, in fact," enthuses the narrator, "that whenever we meet other hikers or fall in with our fellow guests back at the chalet, we feel ashamed to have been admitted to a place from which nobody, in principle, comes back alive. For we come back alive from these conversations with death."

"What does she look like?" inquires Fanny. "Well," says the narrator, "she's just like the picture on the tarot card." "She's that skinny?" asks Fanny. "Oh yes, and she can't even be called skinny: *emaciated* is the word. She's that skeleton depicted by all those who have seen her and conversed with her at length." "She's a woman, right?" asks Fanny, who has herself seen something of this kind. "Yes, she's a woman, of course, I can confirm that," replies the narrator. "At her feet, if I'm not mistaken, are half-buried bodies," adds Fanny, a stickler for accuracy. "What's her voice like? Is it bleak?" "Her voice is companionable," explains the narrator. "I couldn't begin to describe her qualities. You see, Fanny, when I walk with her in the mountains, I feel a sense of companionship that no one else in the world gives me." "Are you never frightened of her?" asks Fanny. "Aren't you afraid of brushing against her, for example?" "I avoid doing so," replies her friend. "I walk at a respectful distance so that there's never any risk of my touching her. No, I never feel scared. Our meetings are harmless and controlled by fate, as we both know. And I would add this, dear Fanny: the company of a narrator might even be of some comfort to her, for in any other circumstance she is obliged to go about her work. I've noticed in her, at times, a certain weariness at forever reaping, reaping. I grant her a respite, a period of rest." "But, narrator, can you intercede?" asks Fanny. "Ask her to spare such and such a person, for example?" "No, I can't do that," the narrator replies. "She mows down whomever she wants, she's unrelenting, she goes her way. But, yes, Fanny, I think, I think and I feel, that she's in no great rush to mow down the ones I love."

Fanny and the narrator make their way through the woods surrounding the country asylum devoutly, like does. Fanny is wearing a red dress from which her slender brown arms emerge, and at the tip of one of those arms her right hand—her writing hand—which she clenches and unclenches continuously to exercise the muscles, for a few years back it was cut open in an accident that destroyed the nerves and atrophied the muscles. Fanny was advised to exercise it continuously, so she exercises it continuously. With this right hand, she picks flowers for the narrator and offers them to him. He tears off a pretty strip of bark from a tree and offers it to her. They exchange primitive gifts like beings who lack a common language, or rather, who refuse to believe in the effectiveness of language—which is always illusory—and have reverted to exchanging gifts to convey that they mean well, no longer wish to murder each other, and would like to stay in touch.

Sometimes, a man or a woman wanders by who in two or three sentences Fanny describes to the narrator. "Why do you describe them to me with such skill and panache?" he asks. "You know I'm a narrator, you know how enthralling—and how moving—I find it when you describe your friends to me." "I know," says Fanny. "It's as though you were telling me a story so that I can tell a story," the narrator goes on. "What do you think?" "No," says Fanny, wavering. "Of course, I know for you it's all grist to the mill, but I tell stories in the same way to others." She evades the issue, refusing to discuss it further while continuing to deliver up with insane generosity stories so intoxicating that the narrator could fall asleep in one of them. She tells him about P., who is forever clamoring for respect by showing off his immense learning, but can't fall asleep at night if his blanket has not been tucked in properly. R., fifty years of age, who phones her mother six times a day, knows she shouldn't but is unable to cut the cord. V., who everyone is very sweet to, Fanny says, acts and speaks like a child of three. G., who only gets on well with cats, cannot speak to her fellow men, but is on such good terms with cats that they reply to her. F. never goes anywhere without a mirror so that he can examine himself in another mirror and try to catch a glimpse of whatever's "in the back of his mind." "It's too much for me," sighs the narrator. "I'm not sure I'd be able to give an account of it all."

Fanny's role is so strange, muses the narrator. Her whole predicament, in fact. What on earth is she doing in this madhouse when she's not herself mad, just frail in the face of cruelty, indifference, brutality? You'd think she was a spy, observing this alien world and wondering if she would be better off here or in the other, the brutal and pitiless one. "Choose," the narrator tells her. "And choose, I beg you, the world of the living. You have a body, you're pretty and you know so many things. Believe me, Fanny, you will be loved." But Fanny wavers, tempted in one direction, tempted in the other. And it's this wavering that makes her an ideal friend in the narrator's eyes. "God knows, I managed to choose," he says sheepishly. "To side with the living, the two-faced, the heartless, the pitiless, but protected by my secret function in life. What else could I do? Protect yourself, Fanny, protect yourself with a secret. Don't tell everything, don't show the world the beauty of your anxious soul. Learn to play, learn to show the world only what it's willing to accept in the way of mediocrity, and keep your beauty for yourself and your friends." She listens. She wants to stand naked before the world and be accepted or rejected for what she is. "The Madame Saintiers will kill you," the narrator tells her. "Too bad," says Fanny, who's incapable of lying.

XI

WITH MADAME SAINTIER, IT'S DONE: they're in love. The narrator, no matter how close an eye he keeps on himself or how often he tries to mend his ways, cannot help but pursue his secret goals. He's in love, then — so it seems — with Madame Saintier, that is to say he desires her, she desires him and together they make frenzied love, as though searching for the answer to a question that has no answer. From time to time, he thinks of relinquishing his role as a narrator. He toys with the idea. Madame Saintier plays along with him. Were he to insist, for example, that Madame Saintier get a divorce so that he can live with her, he would cease to be a narrator and become a husband, which merits consideration.

He imagines not being a narrator. It's tempting. He's a grown man at last. He puts away the diseased part of his brain, stops wanting to wield power, ceases to have a secret, and, when he's walking in the countryside, takes a serious interest in flowers, plants, geography, archeology, history. He's willing to look ridiculous when chatting with someone who knows more about something than he does—he isn't panic-stricken at feeling ridiculous. For Madame Saintier he makes one, then two, then four children, and he doesn't play weird games with them; he puts his fantasies to one side and sets about raising the children properly. He shuts down his mental echo chamber. Like Véronique, Alain and Patricia, he has boundaries he will not cross. There are things, he declares, he has no wish to know, because like his friends he realizes that this is the only way to keep on top of things and stay sane. When he travels he does so intelligently, not in order to reengage with his dark, orgasmic dreams, but to learn useful, sterling things: a foreign language, a country's social and political situation. Basically, he tells himself, I've sought nothing but enjoyment all these years.

I need to love someone who's not at all my type.

Someone stronger than me, someone better informed and more skilled than I am in my line of work. I need to find a supreme narrator. He casts about but finds no one, since the moment a supreme narrator comes along, he recoils in fright and hides in a corner. Well, well … he says to himself, it's not force I dread, so much as competition … Someone as innocent as myself, up to my neck in rivalry? Anxious never to put myself in a situation where I wouldn't be top dog? Well, I never …

You cut a sorry figure, narrator, you're neither the noble Don Quixote nor noble at all. You're a bit lame, in fact. But since we are good-natured and hospitable, we who have no name, we who are the name you seek but have still not found, we're going to give you a hand. Perhaps. Or perhaps not. For the first time in your life, you're beginning to feel a little less fearful, right? From now on, my friend, you've got to listen to us. You've got to stop playing your lousy tricks. "But will I still have fun?" sniffles the narrator. For starters, stop acting like a child. It won't work. "And what about my sorry figure?" groans the narrator. "It's remained so youthful and prepossessing that people always think I'm ten years younger than I am. It makes me so happy! Do I really have to …" Yes. Grow old. Stop clutching at your miserable, new-blown youth. Stop playing all these tricks, because if you carry on like this you'll be in for a fall. A big one." "Very well," says the narrator, who has found his master, "I'm ready. What do I have to do? Where do I have to go? Can I bring a suitcase? Will I need a change of clothes? And how long will I be gone? Can I say goodbye to my friends? Will I be allowed to go and kiss them, and even Monsieur Saintier, who after all ..." Stop making such a fuss.

XII

TO TAKE STOCK OF HIS BOOKS, THOUGHTS and remarks and make sure they're not confined solely to the affluent classes, the narrator sometimes goes to visit the poor quarter of this or that city, where he encounters hunched bodies and tired, leaden faces. These are the measuring rods he employs to gauge his sentences. Faced with this sad, slow man doing his shopping or this anxious young mother, he asks himself: "Does my book also say something about you? Does it take your existence into account? Does it say anything of your thoughts, your preoccupations, your emotions? Does it somehow do you justice?" The answer is highly uncertain. Much of the time it seems to him: no, neither his book nor his conscience has taken these poor, tired people into account. And, as he makes his way back uptown and comes across people who are increasingly well-dressed, with fewer and fewer worries, with rested faces and well-groomed bodies, he no longer has anything to measure his book against.

So he goes back. And very often, faced with a man or a woman with an embittered mouth and a slow step, he says to himself despairingly that he might just as well throw his book away when he gets home. He doesn't feel for these people the sympathy he feels for the lunatics with their astonishing speech, yet in their company he throws off his oversized narrator's outfit like a coat that is much too heavy, and only then does he have the impression of belonging to the human race. He stops playing to the gallery. He stops pretending to be in love. He makes his way along the sidewalk without ceremony, without gloating, without puffing out his chest. He walks gravely at their side, musing that one day he will die and these people will die with him. Were he to fall here among them, were he to collapse in a heap on the sidewalk, which is covered this summer with beautiful, aniseed-colored pollen, they wouldn't cry out or make a fuss. They would call an ambulance perhaps, without saying much. He's tempted to fall here among them. Were he to fall one day, he would like it to be among them.

In the meantime, there's his great story to be told. And there are moments when the landscape's demand for the story is so vociferous as to be deafening. No matter where the narrator is walking, he can never find rest, since the rivers gleaming white in the sun and the haughty, high trees, the landlocked lakes and slender branches, the immovable summits and seemingly blameless meadows are all in conversation with him, demanding he intervene, in the same way that someone who is deeply unhappy will sit before you in grim-faced silence, hoping with all his soul that you will find the word that will free him to tell his story.

Whenever the narrator sits down by a green lake or a tall tree and is sad, as he is just now, the two of them—the lake and the narrator, or the tree and the narrator—remain there without speaking for quite some time. "Come on," the narrator eventually pipes up, since he's accustomed to speaking in public: "Instead of gaping at one another like stuck pigs, why don't we try talking . . ." The leaves on the tree stir; a breath of wind ruffles the surface of the lake. "I don't like these power games," lets slip the narrator, flinging a pebble into the water. "I beg you, you might at least look at me." And it's now that—for all his sorrow and his many defeats, and despite the absence of proof that weighs on him like a verdict handed down by some mysterious court—he starts to sing the story for the tenth, the hundredth time. The words come in droves, clumsy, enchanted, nudging their way with difficulty through the nonconducting block of the narrator's grief. But he has his herd under control, the narrator; he's skilled, he knows his animals and how to call them.

Very weak that day, having just come back from the lake and his conversation with the trees, but having advanced a little all the same, just a few sentences, the narrator scans the countryside in search of a kindly presence. But of course! here she is, it's Madame Saintier, walking in the mountains, searching for him perhaps, and bringing him sandwiches and something to drink. "I hope I'm not disturbing you," she says, a little out of breath and laden with victuals like a mother at teatime, "but I thought . . ." Oh my, how weak he is! And nobody has noticed a thing! She hands him the bottle and he drinks from it like a teat. The weight of the teat is almost too heavy for his lips. She hands him a sandwich and he bites into it, unable to say a word. Seated beside him without touching him — heaven forbid, he would drop dead were someone to touch him now, and she understands this perfectly! — she pulls her skirt down over her knees and, narrowing her eyes, gazes into the distance without speaking.

Gradually he feels the warmth returning. His body, threatened with extinction, slowly comes back to life. He can say a few words now, and it's getting easier to drink from the bottle. She remains silent. The story continues to arrive. They spend a long evening by the water's edge: she, who has understood everything and no longer wishes to murder him, quite the contrary; he, who has still not learned to love but feels able now to be loved, succored, assisted, on the strict understanding that there can be no word for this. Devotedly, she waits for him to speak first. She could wait like this for a hundred years without showing the least sign of impatience. He knows this, he can feel it, and is deeply grateful to her. Little by little, then, as his body slowly comes back to life and the blood once more begins to circulate in his deadened limbs, in the same way that he had grown taller and taller and stronger and stronger by chasing after his mother, he ceases to be an infant at the breast and is three, then seven, then twelve, then seventeen, then twenty-seven, and lo! he's a grown man. Drinking from the bottle becomes very easy, swallowing the sandwich, too, and then speaking, as he says to her: "We should go now. It's getting chilly." How proud he is to be able to place his arm around this woman's shoulders!

They make their way up through the fields. Aware that the narrator is prone to bouts of depression, and knowing how to avoid triggering one, she's still mindful not to talk too much, while he, who feels ashamed of his affliction and tries to combat it, seeks cautiously, earnestly to bond with this woman. He says a few words, with a kind of bumbling self-assurance; she knows exactly how to respond, which draws him out. He carries on, a little less awkwardly than before, until their conversation resembles one of those interminable, mantra-like greetings that people in traditional societies exchange, without looking at one another, each time they meet. It's not information they're exchanging, still less are they showing off their wit: it's a ball they're passing between them, a ball they're tossing gently back and forth like two people playing with night and day, while all around them the world achieves the amazing feat of remaining in a state of equilibrium, thanks to their exchange.

This must be what love is, thinks the narrator. How cautious they are! How careful not to clash! It's as though they can only touch one another with intangible things. Yet here is the narrator capable of sitting down behind the steering wheel of a car, and Madame Saintier of snapping in her seat belt with panache. They drive along by the shore of the lake, past the dam and then on through a village like actual human beings, human beings who had gone to spend a pleasant afternoon swimming and lying beside a lake. They swig on a water bottle in the car, where some blue flowers she has picked for him are drying on the back seat. They stop at an inn for a drink. Up it comes, life, up it comes. Most of the narrator's numbness has gone. Even his right hand is working. "My right hand's working again," he says. "That's good," she says.

XIII

HENCEFORTH, HE WOULD MUCH PREFER not to be abandoned by the story, for it does him a world of good, airlifting him so high above the earth that he has the impression of writing like an angel. "I'm going to throw a party," the narrator informs Madame Saintier. "If it's all right with you, I'm going to throw a party at your chalet and invite a few friends, including my great friend Fanny. To bring Fanny to the chalet is to welcome into my heart, in glory, a part of the world I have long kept at arm's length, have long been afraid of—so afraid, in fact, that I would go and hide in a corner to cry. Thanks to you," he tells Madame Saintier, "a happy ending of sorts is taking shape. Because of the boundless hospitality you have shown me at the chalet, because we have fought together in the mountains, because I was terrified of your power, but also because we have stood our ground" (for the first time, the narrator says "we") "and because you have turned your kind eyes on me, Fanny can now leave the country asylum and the edge of the woods where a death that is menacing because you can't communicate with it prowls, and board a train in her red dress from which her skinny, nervous arms emerge."

"This afternoon, we'll go and meet her at the station, you and I. She's about to step ashore on this newfound land where she knows I live and which I have often described to her at length." "Is she curious about it?" asks Madame Saintier. "I don't know," replies the narrator, "at any rate, it's the first time she has agreed to come, perhaps just to make me happy. But I don't suppose she'll stay long. She has other plans. No doubt she'll tell us about them." And the narrator thinks of the sky: will the weather be fine when Fanny arrives? It would be lovely if the sky were soft and blue with a few white clouds. It would be marvelous if it were mild and sunny, something like spring. "I think she'll be bringing spring," he says. Whereupon Madame Saintier (who has never met Fanny) tries on two or three outfits before deciding on the second one, while the narrator rushes about in a frenzy, sprucing up his room and laughing. "But Fanny couldn't care less about tidy little interiors!" he says to himself, laughing even harder. It's noon, then two, then three o'clock. They don't know what to do, Madame Saintier and the narrator, to pass the time. On the station platform, a good thirty minutes before the train is due to arrive, he has the impression of acting out a very ancient scene, of being back in the world of his ancestors, where someone was waiting for someone on a platform one day and something momentous occurred, something that would determine the lives, sufferings and pleasures of generations to come. He's a bit scared. He feels very lonely.

Despite the friendly presence of Madame Saintier, and though he has a little more support than if he had been standing there on his own, he's still alone in the world in waiting for Fanny.

She arrives, and it's spring. In her red dress from which her skinny brown arms emerge, she walks toward them with a smile, holding a small suitcase in her right hand. She doesn't say anything earth-shattering. Oh no, it's way better than that. She says things like: "Yes, I had a pleasant journey." "Are you tired?" asks the narrator with somewhat exaggerated civility. "No, no, just a bit thirsty." Delicately they take their places on metal chairs on a café terrace, and the narrator, overawed by the coming of spring, feels swaying with joy inside him a child's rattle, a carillon of bells.

As they make their way from the café to the chalet, he hears himself showing the sights to Fanny, pointing out a church, a garden, a fountain. She listens, while hanging from her arm is the small, heavy suitcase she doesn't find heavy at all. She's neither hot nor cold, and when you think she's about to laugh, she doesn't, just as when she speaks it's never to say something the narrator had divined in advance. "That's what spring is," he muses, "something continually surprising and always true." He shows her the roundabouts and roads. He talks far too much, of course, but he's feeling a bit emotional. She barely looks at him, and she certainly doesn't touch him with so much as a fingertip, not once. She does something quite remarkable: while he's hastily delivering his little introductions and welcoming addresses, she doesn't once interrupt him. She always responds, but only when he has reached the end of his interminable sentence, and when she disagrees, she does so quietly, gently.

At the chalet, while she goes up to her room to unpack, he retires to his, so excited and so overcome with emotion that he paces around the room four times, smiling and rubbing his hands, straightening a picture, pulling up the blanket, moving an object on the dresser a few inches, then putting it back as it was. He's only half listening. He doesn't want to eavesdrop or spy on her as he does with the other guests, but he can't be altogether deaf, of course, to the coming of spring. Ten minutes, he tells himself, after glancing at his watch. Ten minutes, then I'll go back down. In the meantime, he flings open the window and gazes out at the horizon, which he knows by heart. "Did you buy the house for the view?" he had asked Madame Saintier on his first day there, when he discovered the huge panorama of blue mountains. "Among other things," she had replied.

Fanny's room is at the other end of the chalet. "What's she doing?" he whispers to Madame Saintier, who's making her way silently along the corridor. "She's listening to music, I think," Madame Saintier replies. "Well, I never ..." murmurs the narrator, who rubs his hands and doesn't know quite what to do with his ten fingers, his footsteps, his flaming heart or the timorousness that has taken hold of him since the arrival of spring. As for Fanny, here she is, at suppertime, coming down with great naturalness and simplicity to the dining room. She doesn't realize what an event she is, thinks the narrator. Whenever I'm facing outward in my story, she has her back turned; and when I'm the one with my back turned, she faces outward. Whenever I go off into the mountains, she stays behind, here in the valley; and when she's the one who goes off into the mountains, I'm the one who stays behind. It's a movement that goes on outside us, over which we have no control. She's the other side of my face, as I am of hers. "Relatively speaking," declares Fanny, with just a hint of irony. "Yes, of course, relatively speaking," the narrator repeats hastily, a little shamefaced.

XIV

THE FOLLOWING EVENING, HOWEVER, THE party doesn't at all turn out to his advantage. It's his friends who, like Fanny, had arrived at the chalet the evening before, who begin: "Narrator, don't put us in your story," they say, "we have no wish to be there." If he tries to explain that a story is always collective, that they are necessarily involved in putting it together: "Well, in that case," they declare rudely, "we may not wish to remain friends with you any longer. For you see, narrator, we have our own lives and thoughts, our own feelings, every bit as delicate as yours, if not more so, and to find ourselves turned into forms which, I can assure you, bear very little resemblance to ourselves, is most unpleasant. We have no wish, narrator, to be turned into characters. We loathe the idea of becoming characters." "That's only natural," murmurs the narrator. "But without you, I'm dead." "At least change our names," protests Alain. "I don't remember saying that," murmurs Madame Saintier. "It's really not fair," declares Fanny, "that I and others whom you claim so fervently to love are the very people you fleece. You're a wolf, narrator, and I detest your story. What on earth were you thinking when you set me down in a 'country asylum'? Who do you take me for? How dare you turn me into a sort of paper puppet!" "But that's the whole point," mumbles the narrator, "it's not you I have painted, it's an image that you call to mind." "And this body you describe. How dare you describe my body and my arms and my hands!" exclaims Fanny. "Because sometimes I bore that body," grumbles the narrator. "Oh you did, did you? And why exactly did you bear it? So that you could make use of it perhaps? So that you could take possession of it? "Perhaps," says the narrator.

"Perhaps I do nothing cleanly. Perhaps, in spite of myself, I can only act inside a book."

The hour of judgment has come. They're seated in a circle in Madame Saintier's sitting room, and the narrator is of two minds: is he willing to die, or alternatively, can he face losing them all? He's willing to grant a few concessions, but not all of them: to say a green dress instead of a red dress, or Pierre instead of Alain, or Madame Vent instead of Madame Saintier … But that's not what they're asking him to do. What they're asking him to do is to throw away his book. It's only fair. "There *is* a way," he suggests pitifully, "and that would be for you not to read me." It's such a silly idea that nobody answers. "For heaven's sake!" he exclaims, "do I once show you in a ridiculous, pitiful or pathetic light?" "On such and such a page," one of them declares, "you say that you're surrounded exclusively by losers, which is not exactly a compliment since I'm part of that group." "And what about me!" cries out Yvan, "whom you pretended to like and had so many conversations with, you make me look like an idiot!" "But I really did enjoy talking to you," says the narrator, in a sweat, "and that's precisely why I was able to seize on certain ingredients …" "Ingredients, I ask you …" scowls Patricia. "Why have you only pointed up our weaknesses and failings? We have our good points, too, you know!" And she bursts into tears.

"Quite right," Fanny chimes in, "you describe all of us solely in terms of our weaknesses. That, narrator, is what is unacceptable. Your book is a way of seizing power, and by the same token, an attempt to destroy us." "And when you do describe our qualities," Madame Saintier pitches in, "you're so supercilious and patronizing that they come across as ridiculous and pitiful!" "I think we'll have to kill him," someone remarks. "Or at least get him to write another book," says another, a little alarmed by the turn events are taking. "Write another book? You know full well that's impossible!" groans the narrator. "Each book has first of all to be written, and then made public, in order for the next one to be born. If you bury this one, what will become of me? Two years' misery, back to square one, trying to think differently, without your …" "So what?" says someone devoid of compassion, "what's two years' misery to us?"

He's tempted to throw away his book. What's a book, after all, compared to life or your loved ones' feelings? Some passages he likes—the one about death, for example. No one will object to death. And the one about babies. What baby would ever criticize him for mentioning him? Or the poor people in the sad neighborhoods whom he was tempted to collapse in a heap among in the aniseed-colored pollen: they won't pick a quarrel with him. They don't read. Only those who don't read can love me, thinks the narrator. Which is a bit odd. And those who aren't acquainted with me in one form or another, who don't know me. It makes for an odd sort of company. It doesn't really make for company at all.

They haven't killed him yet this evening, so the narrator will spend the night asking himself why he's so intent on describing people's weaknesses. "Perhaps it's because it's what I know best," he tells himself. A bit lame. "Perhaps it's because, at bottom, hardship is all there is in life." Not true. There are the heroes, my friend, the ones who are stronger than you, the ones who don't drag a numb limb behind them all the time, the alpha narrators. Where are they? The narrator, wavering: "Well ... they're on my bookshelves ..." No! thunders the voice. I'm talking about the living, your contemporaries. Who do you admire? Who has created a perfect world? "Well now ... There's so-and-so ... And then there's that fellow ..." Their names! "No! I refuse to mention their names in a work of fiction!" Oh you do, do you? And you don't mention your friends' names in a work of fiction, I suppose? "It's terrible what you're putting me through," says the narrator. "It's like torture. It's as though you were trying to get me to confess. And not to a crime, which is all too easy to confess to, but to a wish, a jealousy, which is distinctly less so." But you're getting warm, aren't you? "Yes, I'm getting warm," concedes the narrator, as his coat falls to the floor.

"OH, PLEASE LET ME CHEAT," HE IMPLORES.
"Please let me cheat, again and again. Let me run
along behind my mother once more! It was so marvelous, the ecstasy I felt—unheard-of, and so bracing that I felt like a torrent, a mountain spring! Let
me talk to the lakes and trees, let me tell people the
story, and may they love me for recounting such desirable things! Don't prevent me from feeling glad
and dominant with the lunatics, the ramblers, the
friends I choose for myself. I feel so forlorn if instead
of being invisible I go unnoticed; you know that. I
was made that way, my friend. There's nothing anyone can do about it, there's nothing I can do about it,
I can't seriously wish to be anything but a narrator,
because I simply don't have the means. I've tried to
take an interest in history, politics, other people. I
swear I have struggled with all my might, as all of us
narrators have. But I just can't do it. My brain lacks
the wherewithal. Suppose I were to heed your sum-
mons: what would happen? I would die, that's what.
And I don't want to die, or not right this second at
least. I want to go on having fun, go on having more
and more fun. Shudder to feel myself so alone, go up
into the mountains, throb with the knowledge of my
invisibility." The other, who is seated opposite the
narrator, very tall and very broad, a commanding

presence, doesn't say a word. Might it be that he's keeping silent before delivering the final blow? wonders the narrator. Or might he be shaken to the core?

"I promise you I'll pay more attention from now on," continues the narrator, who's growing younger by the minute. Lo! he's no longer forty, but thirty, twenty, ten: "Look!" he says, as he pulls some books from his pocket. "I'm going to learn another language! I'm going to travel! And not, I swear, in order to reengage with my orgasmic dreams, but to … I don't know … to bond with my fellow men, for example." "Yes," he says proudly, "I'm going to try and bond with my fellow men, then you'll see!" But with these words, the forbidding presence, who earlier had appeared to be shrinking, to be shaken to the core and shedding a bit of his self-assurance, puffs out his chest once again, this time in a truly terrifying manner. "No, no!" cries the narrator. "Of course I'll never bond with my fellow men, I'm done for, we know I'm done for. But, hey! I know, I'll adopt a child!' The Presence is even more puffed up. "No, of course I won't adopt a child, it would be madness. But …" (imploring once again) "I beg you, let me lie down once more among the flowers, in a meadow high up in the mountains, and there, hum the same syllables over and over. Let me lie there, my friend, in my cradle and hum to myself until the great opening, until I'm snatched away and swallowed up, and then rise up afresh, start humming again, be swallowed up again, then rise up afresh. Let me gaze at the sky, fill my lungs with the scent of wild thyme, rub the long grass between my fingers."

Sensing that the Great Presence is shaken and growing weak at these words, he carries on like this for two hours, then ten. I'll mesmerize him, too! he says quietly to himself. He rubs his hands and continues. It's so exciting to have this power, even over him! He's twelve now, then in next to no time, seven: "Oh, how lovely and frightening it was to clamber along the stony path behind my mother! The stones, you know, when they flew up, would knock against my ankles, so I now have a permanently swollen ankle, like Oedipus!" (He laughs.) "But it doesn't matter, it doesn't stop me from making my way, clambering along, even when it's very hot. I can see her long brown legs up there, they're my horizon. She's wearing a blue dress or skirt, the dress is dancing about her knees, it's my horizon. I myself have short legs, of course. I'm small but quite brawny, and since I have these goats clambering all round me, I grab hold of their coarse, oily hair, something that will later become, incidentally (and with a nod to the Power), one of my sexual fantasies. Enough said . . . And then I am three," says the narrator in a tiny little voice. "And when I arrive at the top of the mountain, I can't see her anymore, she has quite simply vanished. I look among the fallen rocks, I turn round and round, but no, I can tell you, my friend, she has well and truly vanished."

But this time, despite the moving plea he has put in, he'll find it much harder to leave it at that. Because, all of a sudden, at the end of the book, people start to emerge from the shadows in their full reality. "But have I never loved anyone in that case?" the narrator says to himself with fright. "When I thought I loved someone, was I simply blowing bubbles? What I need to do is experience other people's suffering, the suffering they have in common, the thing that makes them stand before you in earnest without smiling or showing off their wit. The thing that gives them such weary bodies and eyes at times." Heavens, he almost feels fit to join them! And what a marriage that will be. Soon perhaps, when he's strolling about, he'll be able to feel on the same level with them all. Soon perhaps, he'll step into a different dream, *their* dream, and how marvelous it will be to be on an equal footing at last. Nothing will scare him anymore, he'll speak the same language as they do and he'll no longer have a secret. At last, he'll no longer have a secret!

How good it feels to be rid of his narrator's outfit! What a relief it is! He's so glad not to be hamstrung anymore! Here he is, then, more or less naked. He no longer plays around, but he does align his brain differently, trying with all his might to point it in the right direction, the direction of life. The outsize brain rebels. The narrator sets to work like a journey-man, a laborer. And, needless to say, ringing urgently, stridently inside him all the while, like an emergency call, is the following question: would you really like to stop being a writer? And the madman answers yes.

THE WISHING TABLE

I WAS SEVEN THE FIRST TIME I SAW MY FATHER dressed as a girl. I was on my way home when I saw a woman coming toward me on the sidewalk in red platform sandals, with a long summer coat, maybe silk, or something glossy at any rate, billowing out behind her. But what really struck me was her ruffled, bleached-blonde hair, the gigantic earrings flapping about her neck, her eyelids spangled with aquamarine glitter. She was terrifying, like Laura Van Bing in *Crucifixion* or Crusoe Kiki in her "frenzied dance."

I didn't recognize him straightaway, since he usually wore a jacket. One day, I had caught Marjorie Higgins pressing the entire length of her body against him in the hallway, and he had given her a good slap. Quite right, too, I thought. Another time, I overheard Marjorie confessing to my mother that she had once made an "inappropriate gesture," an indiscretion she could no longer hide from her because Maman was such a dear old friend. Maman burst out laughing, they hugged each other, and their breasts brushed together as they embraced.

Maman was naked most of the time. "You have no shame," Papa would say. She would stand in front of the hall mirror, combing her bush with the same thoroughness and gusto with which she brushed her teeth at night. One of my classmates was astounded by this: "Your mother is naked!" she said to me with a gasp. "Yes," I replied, "we have no shame in our family." Later, she liked to come visit just so that she could see Maman seated naked in front of the living-room window, or watering the flowers, her voluptuous breasts swaying gently back and forth.

If you want to know what my mother looked like, which is what everyone asks me when I tell this story, here is a brief description: she was twenty-eight, with pale skin and long fair hair, which she wore loose, streaming down her back. She was a "girl from the North." Taller than Marjorie, she had a soft white body and long thighs. Constantly worried that she was getting fat, she would examine herself in every mirror in the house, then turn to me and say, "Don't you think I've put on weight, sweetie?" She would clutch her belly in both hands, squeezing it together, and groan: "My God, what a gut! I'm getting really fat!" And I would say, "Oh, come on, you're not fat, you're a sylph" because the insurance agent had once told her, "Marianne, you're so beautiful. You're positively sylphlike!" and I had seen from the little smile she gave that it had pleased her.

Maman was probably what you'd call an "exhibitionist," as Dr. Mars said later. Even when she did wear clothes, her nightgown would drift open or her stockings would come free from their garters. She was always having to pull up her skirt to clip them back on. Her blouses were a stitch too tight, so that the top button might pop off at any moment. She seemed very much in love with Papa, but he was hard on her. The moment he was home, she would plead with him, "Touch me! Touch me, my love!" while they sat watching television together on the sofa. Whereupon Papa would brutally squeeze one of her breasts, or, without glancing around, tug violently at the curls of her bush.

They did things with us that it's absolutely forbidden to do with children. Especially Maman, who loved to fondle us. She just had to see our pussies, to touch and rub us, to "gamahuche" us, as they say in Sade. Around three in the afternoon, she would call out, "Come to me, I'm on fire!" She would drape herself across an armchair, her long thighs spread wide, and Chloe, Ingrid or I, or all three at once, would set about tickling her, nibbling at her, rubbing, pinching, and licking her. When Papa was present, he would seize the opportunity, not to touch Maman, who would gaze imploringly at him with her dark brown eyes, but to have his way with us instead. His penis was obviously huge.

Perhaps because of our family activities — it's what Dr. Mars thought — we reached puberty very early on, my sisters and me, around ten or eleven. Maman was delighted when she discovered our budding breasts and the first sparse patches of pubic hair. "You'll see just how much you're going to enjoy life from now on." She and Marjorie would excitedly massage our chests, placing bets on which of us would turn out to be the most voluptuous, probing our pussies and behinds with their fingers. "Of the three, I think Ingrid will be the most disposed to sodomy," said Marjorie. Papa thought so, too, and would retire with Ingrid to his study whenever Maman got on his nerves with her frenzied love for him.

II

OUR PARENTS WEREN'T SO DUMB AS TO imagine the whole world would approve of our way of life. There was almost a scandal the time my school friend saw Maman combing herself in the mirror. For a week or two, the girl said nothing. She was desperate to see Maman naked again, looking forward to it whenever she came to visit, but in the end she couldn't contain herself. She told her brother, who told their parents, and from then on she was forbidden to set foot in the house or so much as speak to me. At school, they made me see a psychologist, who asked me questions and had me make some drawings. I drew a few flowers, a few trees, and told him that no, Maman did not walk around naked.

Dr. Mars was one of our allies. Whenever he stopped by, always in a mad rush between two house calls, he would follow Maman into the dining room, shove her down against the table and thrust himself violently inside her. But apart from a few family friends—I've mentioned Marjorie Higgins, the insurance agent and Dr. Mars, and I'll come to Pierre Peloup, Myriam de Choiseul, and the Vinssé brothers soon—we kept to ourselves.

III

WHEN I FIRST SAW PAPA, ON JULY 7, 1967, walking up the rue Alban-Berg dressed as a girl— for I recognized him eventually—I was amazed and wanted to follow him, which I did on several occasions. He would make his way past the small front gardens on the rue Alban-Berg to the crossroads, and from there leave our residential neighborhood for the town center. He would go into all the boutiques, trying out perfumes, clothes and a vast array of underwear. Sometimes he would go and sit in a café, sometimes a movie theater, and he would regularly stop a man or a woman passing by to ask them something—the location of a street, say, when in fact he knew every corner of the city like the back of his hand. People would turn and stare at him as he walked by. He loved that. The one time he saw me, he reverted to his man's voice and told me to scram. He would arrive home tired after having walked all that way in such narrow shoes. Maman, all but kneeling before him, would slip them off and lick his feet. She was always doing things like that.

IV

YOU PROBABLY THINK WE HAD TO BE REALLY messed up, living as we did in what other people would have called "moral squalor." And you'd be mistaken. Our grades at school were fine, and we were on excellent terms with our friends. For nothing comes more easily to a child than lying; it's his world, in fact, the one where he swims most freely and fares best. True, when Maman gazed up at Papa with her wild, animal eyes and he refused to gratify her insatiable desires, when she was burning with lust, waiting for Marjorie or Dr. Mars to come and set her free, when she threw herself on us and rubbed us so hard that we nearly fainted, the atmosphere in the house was tense. But the tension was part of the pleasure, something we were born to. We had no taste for the comforts of life, which bored us, and on the rare, the very rare occasions — it was most unusual, but it did sometimes happen — when Maman would put on a dress and sit by the window sewing, when our bodies had been left unattended, when Dr. Mars was away and the insurance agent had gone off on vacation, we would become fretful and start to feel the first stirrings of despair, and we were the ones then who turned into wild beasts, looking for a wrist to lick or a sex to devour. A handout, a pittance, anything!

V

THIS IS WHAT HAPPENED WHEN WE WENT on holiday to our grandparents' cottage in Tremble. They shared neither our parents' morals, nor their views on life, and we would get horribly bored in their house in August. Papa and Maman had to be very careful, very discreet. Maman was never naked. She went around in a dress, sighing. Papa never dressed up as a girl. We would dart imploring glances their way, which, since they were furtive, met with no response but were waved aside with a superior air.

In the afternoon, we would go off in the car under the pretense of doing a bit of sightseeing or swimming on some beach, at which point what can only be called "our family life" would start up again for two or three hours. The moment we pulled out of the driveway, Maman would tear off her dress and sit naked in the front seat, her face convulsed with passion and pressed up against the window for the benefit of the other motorists. Papa would change clothes at the first turnoff, and we would learn afresh how to fondle each other and copulate like beasts. We would come back less agitated, even if we missed the environment of our own home, the visits from Dr. Mars, the assurances of the insurance agent, and the sight of Maman vigorously combing herself in the mirror.

VI

WE WOULD SPEND THE WHOLE OF AUGUST IN Tremble, returning home on September 1st. Oh, September 1st! On the eve of our departure, we'd be champing at the bit! The sun, the fresh air, the beach and the countryside had kept us so much apart that we didn't know where we were. Our little house on the rue Alban-Berg, with its polished furniture and the dining-room table where Maman would recline, Papa's study, which we never tired of entering, and the hallway with the huge mirror in which Maman would examine her naked reflection—how we longed to be back there! We would arrive home, and an hour later Dr. Mars would turn up with flowers, so hard that he was bursting his trousers, and Papa would rush out dressed as a girl, even if it was a Sunday.

VII

FOR MY TENTH BIRTHDAY, AS THOUGH I HAD reached an "age of reason," Maman introduced the insurance agent, Dr. Mars, Pierre Peloup, Myriam de Choiseul, Marjorie, and the Vinssé brothers into our love feasts. I particularly remember Pierre Peloup because he had a liking for me, whereas Dr. Mars, though he didn't by any means look down his nose at us, preferred Maman, and the insurance agent enjoyed threesomes with Papa and Ingrid. I don't know why, as she was pretty, but Chloe was less attractive to them, at least back then.

Pierre Peloup was an optician, which is how we came to meet him. Maman needed corrective lenses for her myopia, and I went along with her. Pierre

Peloup looked like a wolf, with his small sharp white teeth, his red lips always frozen in a half smile, his gleaming eyes and his thick black hair. He must have been around thirty-five. Maman thrust her breasts out the whole time she was trying out the lenses, so that the straps of her dress slid down off her shoulders and hung loose around her arms; and as she was breathing heavily and staring at him through a lens that made her eye look enormous, he was powerless to resist. When he came to the house, he was a little uneasy, like everyone the first time they came round—everyone who wasn't part of our family, I mean. Maman had opened the door to him naked and was particularly beautiful that day, having rubbed her bush with an oil that gave it a tawny, animal glow. Her breasts were more voluptuous than ever, she had even rouged her nipples. I stood behind her in the hallway, as she had asked me to do. He was speechless, of course, but when he saw Maman's beautiful behind passing ahead of him into the dining room, he quickly came to his senses.

Sometimes Maman had these little flights of fancy, "which only added to her charm," as Dr. Mars remarked. That first time with Pierre Peloup, she absolutely insisted on sitting me down on her lap, my face pressed against her breasts, and while I sucked on one nipple, Pierre Peloup sucked on the other. Maman was extremely sensitive: wherever you touched her, whatever part of her body you caressed, she enjoyed it. Her fingers were playing with my pussy, while Pierre Peloup had pulled out his sex and was entertaining us with it: it was perhaps thanks to this first encounter that he had so much pleasure with me later.

Maman let me go out alone with him. I would climb into his car, which was parked a few streets over from ours — he didn't want people to know he was a regular visitor to our home — and we would head out into the countryside. He loved the countryside; or perhaps it wasn't that, perhaps he just liked being alone with me in the countryside. We would always stop by the same canal, beneath some beautiful trees, a long way from the last houses, an ideal spot from which we could make out even the haziest of silhouettes for several hundred yards in any direction. And there he would come on my face, my body, my hands as they squeezed him, or inside me. At the beginning, he was always promising to bring me dolls or toys or a million other stupid things. The promises ceased when he finally understood that I didn't need any incentive to drive out into the countryside with him.

You could say that Pierre Peloup was my first lover, after Papa. Dr. Mars, though he enjoyed touching us, didn't penetrate us until later. He liked having us around when he was mounting Maman from behind. He relished our presence in the dining room with the

big polished table, Ingrid, Chloe and me, or sometimes only one of us, a bit like the little naked cher-
ubs that surround a Madonna in glory (with Maman,
of course, in the role of the Madonna.) So we were
present at their lovemaking—which was often hur-
ried, as Dr. Mars was always in a rush between house
calls—seated in an armchair or under the table, if that
was what he wanted, or else lending him a hand if he
was having difficulties that day, which wasn't often
the case. Sometimes we'd present our backsides or
pussies to him, or offer him our mouths, but his own
hands or mouth or sex would pass quickly over them.

Maman was beautiful when she was with Dr. Mars.
"I'm inordinately fond of him," she would say. "He
has only to set foot in the hall, you see, and I'm on
fire, in tears, burning, I instantly feel like I'm a cello."
But Maman was in that state pretty much every time
a visitor knocked on the door. She'd had an unhappy
childhood; she needed a bit of madness.

VIII

I STILL HAVEN'T TOLD YOU WHAT OUR HOUSE
was like, because I was under the impression that
the people I was telling my story to were interested
principally in our sex life, and only incidentally in the
other aspects of our existence. But I'll tell you about

it anyway, because I loved it. The house was a bit like Eva Lone's. You came in through a garden that had no great charm, but it was ours. It lacked charm because it wasn't full of those flowers and tall trees and hedgerows that make a garden beautiful. To tell the truth, it was more of a courtyard really, covered with gravel and closed off by an iron gate set into a low wall. There were short strips of lawn to either side of the path, and a flower bed running along the walls of the house where a few flowers eked out an existence. There was no greenery to shelter beneath in summer, not a single tree, which was why we spent so little time there. It made us feel idle and unproductive.

You entered the house by way of a short flight of steps that opened onto a dark, tiled hall. We loved the hall: summer and winter, we would glide across its tiled floor as though skating on an ice rink on razor-sharp blades. To the left there was a coatrack, an umbrella stand, a marble-topped sideboard in dark mahogany, then a tall, mirrored armoire where Maman would inspect herself. Off to the right of the hall was the dining room, almost entirely taken up by a huge table, always freshly polished and shining like a frozen lake. It was there, as I've said, that we went about our affairs. A few seats and chairs were placed around the table perilous. In a corner next to the window were Maman's armchair and sewing table, though there wasn't much light for her to work by as the window was tiny and the room received very little daylight. On the other side of the hall was Papa's study, which was much more comfortable, with thick rugs, shelves filled with books, and better lighting, though often as not he would draw the curtains when we went in there with him. Behind the study was a small kitchen, but Maman was too taken up with her follies to devote much time to cooking or gardening. In general we ate poorly, just a cracker and a piece of pâté, and sometimes not at all. You couldn't say we ever lived a life of luxury in our house, except when one of our friends came over with food from the delicatessen, bottles of wine, chocolates and dessert for a dinner party.

Upstairs, Maman and Papa's room consisted of a large bed, beautiful curtains and a dresser which Maman would rummage through nervously. The room was always a mess, with heaps of mismatched stockings and socks, and underwear dangling from armrests and the backs of chairs, crumpled panties and socks and dresses strewn about the floor. Spilled out across the dresser were her toiletries and cosmetics: traces of powder and overturned perfume bottles. What a contrast with the frozen, shining sobriety of the dining room, where I never once found a speck of dust! Or with Papa's study, so comfortable and cheerful, so pleasurable and well lit. But I suppose we must have liked the contrast. A house that's uniformly comfortable is every bit as boring, I think, as a house that's uniformly solemn or uniformly chaotic. Our house, needless to say, was like a body or a soul: here it had its pockets of chaos, there its lakes of calm; here its icy detachment, there its velvet depths.

I've been asked many times, since I began telling this story, what sort of relationship I had with my sisters. To my mind, Ingrid and Chloe were probably like the two profiles you see when you look at yourself in a three-sided mirror. We were the same and not quite the same. Our closeness in age brought us together, but I don't recall ever enjoying with them the kind of hushed conversations or close-knit loyalties that traditionally bind siblings together. We certainly weren't foes: our family has always abhorred and rejected all forms of hatred, perhaps owing to those carnal ties that bound us so closely together. In saying this, I wouldn't want to appear to be justifying sexual relations with one's family. I know only too well that it's a sensitive issue. But since I've decided to tell my life story, trying to set down as precisely as possible what I felt in that situation, which was obviously dysfunctional and yet functioned so well, no one is going to convince me to tear my hair out, to cover my head with ashes and weep. Because deep down, no one is weeping. On the contrary: everyone is laughing and calling out for a dance.

IX

PAPA'S SEX DELIGHTED US. WE COULD NEVER get enough of looking at it, touching it. Exemplary in form, it stood out with such authority, the pleasures it dispensed were so keen, that I remember the rug woven with large flowers in his study as a garden far superior to anything by Le Nôtre. Papa wielded it with a degree of brutality that enchanted us. Maman had her madness and the wonderful smoothness of her soft, white body; Papa, his gravity and brutality. As I've already said, for a long time Ingrid was his favorite, but this didn't mean he was averse to shutting himself away in the study with Chloe or me from time to time. Papa would pound away at us, a bit like Dr. Mars with Maman, only less rushed, leaving more time for our mutual pleasure. We became so partial to his attentions, I remember, that in 1970 and 1971 in particular, even though we were in awe of his anger—he didn't like to be disturbed— time and again we would go and knock softly on the study door, fretful, hungry for the pleasure that no one else—not Dr. Mars nor Pierre Peloup nor the Vinssé brothers—could give us to quite the same degree. At times we would find ourselves in a quandary, with Maman crying out from the dining room, clamoring for our presence at the shining table, when we had already made up our minds to go and knock on Papa's door. We would stand without moving in the freezing hallway, barefoot since we were naked, fingers raised ready to knock, while Maman in a voice by turns frenzied, listless and pleading would summon us to join her in the dining room, where she was about to pass out with pleasure. Sometimes Papa would be quicker off the mark, and, after letting us into his study, would throw himself on us like a tiger, while Maman moaned away alone. At other times there was quite a gathering in the house, and what with Dr. Mars pressing Maman down over the shining disc of the dining-room table as he mounted her from behind, Pierre Peloup sliding his member into me in the freezing hallway—the tiles of which, I forgot to mention, were dark green, again like the surface of a lake—and Ingrid taking Papa's sex inside her between the padded walls of his study, we were all—with Chloe lending a hand here and there— perfectly happy.

X

WE HAD OUR NEIGHBORS' SCANDALMON-gering to thank if our happiness was interrupted for a month or two. And, I would also say, their envy. Had we forgotten to draw the curtains one day? Was there a spy in our midst? Had Myriam de Choiseul, never the most disciplined of individuals, found the temptation just too great and unburdened herself at last? Suspicions had been aroused, far worse than those leveled at us during the earlier episode with the psychologist at school. Then someone got it into their head to "notify the authorities," and one afternoon, a social worker showed up at our front door.

Papa wasn't home. Maman was naked and busy in the dining room. It was Ingrid who went to the door when the social worker rang and showed her into Papa's study, which was beyond reproach in every respect. There was no risk she would find any sort of compromising object or racy literature there. (I've neglected to mention it until now, but we did have a certain class.) Maman came out to meet her fully dressed and perfectly composed, since we'd spent the whole morning catering to her needs, and engaged her in the most dazzling conversation.

"I am told," the woman began, "that there is possibly something dysfunctional about your family. I would like to discuss the matter with you and your children."

"Dysfunctional?" Maman exclaimed. "In what way?"

"Well," the social worker went on, ill at ease, "there are some who claim—but they may be mistaken—that in your home there is perhaps too much ... intimacy between the members of your family."

"Intimacy?" Maman's surprise was genuine. As I'm sure you've understood, the idea that anything untoward was going on in the house had simply never occurred to her. She thought that this was what life was like. And who's to say she was wrong? The body we formed with our parents and their friends was so close-knit, the traffic between us so sublime and orderly, that the social worker's words seemed to run up against a smooth, softly curved surface. She had no idea how to make a dent in it.

She would glance down at the bright rug woven with enormous flowers, and she could glimpse through the doorway to the study the dark, polished disc of the lake where our mother would recline, but all she saw was a stark, perfectly dusted, well-kept table. She could hear us chattering innocently upstairs. How could she find a way into this household, where, paradoxically, she had already been admitted?

She asked for a tour of the house, and Maman coldly acquiesced. Wrapped in the dark folds of her dress, she led the social worker upstairs to our parents' room, where Chloe, Ingrid, and I had gone to tidy up a few minutes previously. The beautiful curtains fluttered in front of the half-open window, the plum-colored velvet armchairs were reminiscent of the dining-room table in their almost masculine severity, and the bed was perfectly made up and covered with a floral-pattern quilt. The perfume bottles and makeup were neatly arranged on the dresser, the drawers were closed and the carpet was immaculate. The social worker was taken aback.

"Dysfunctional?" asked Maman.

The social worker asked to see our bedrooms, and that was where we messed up, playing too much at being angels. Each of us was seated at her little desk, revising a lesson or doing her homework, and when Maman came in with her, the three faces that gazed up at her were so untroubled, so lovable, that it was a bit provocative. For the social worker, it was like a slap in the face. It was at this point that she realized we were all in it together.

XI

BECAUSE OF OUR NEIGHBORS' SUSPICIONS, our lives were turned upside down for almost two months, and I look back on this period as one of the saddest of my childhood, though there were others which I'll tell you about later. We could no longer live as we had done in the past. Not a moment went by without someone ringing the doorbell, asking to see us or speak with us. Maman was obliged to go around fully dressed. Dr. Mars came to visit less often—we had tipped him off—and when he did come by, it was on the pretext of examining our throats. He was barely permitted to so much as brush against Maman, who was determined to make a good impression on the social workers, though we could tell she was dying inside. We were used to seeing her on fire, rubbing our bodies against hers each day and marveling at her voluptuous breasts, and now here she was hiding it all from us, taking it all away. We began to get moody, which wasn't like us at all. We would wake up feeling sad, whereas in the past we had always leaped out of bed, excited at the idea of starting another day. Papa pined away in his study, and the disc of the dining-room table was gradually covered with a thin layer of dust where we would trace signs with our fingers.

Sometimes we couldn't take it anymore and would be compelled to make love, albeit on the sly. We would lick Maman's sex for a few minutes, while she was performing her toilette at night. Papa would come up to Ingrid's room, and we would wait timidly in line for the stunning view of his erect member, the moment of contact, the introduction of that awe-inspiring device. But everything had been turned upside down. Papa had *never* come up to see us in our rooms; Maman had *never* comported herself like that in her bathroom. And what of the huge round table like a black lake? And the rug in the study with its sparkling flowers? And the tiled hall that gave us so much pleasure? All were deserted. I know it probably sounds absurd, but I swear to you: it was as though we had lost our homeland.

XII

IT WAS THANKS TO THE VINSSÉ BROTHERS that we finally got out of this scrape. They had come to make a psychological assessment of the family, at the behest of who knows what authority, but it wasn't long before they were driving us out to the country-side, Ingrid, Chloe, and me. Without once mention-ing Pierre Peloup by name, or even his existence, we pointed out the canal to them, on the banks of which we would hold our orgies. Yves and Yvon Vinssé were twins. They looked so much alike that we referred to them as "the Vinssé brothers," since we found them hard to tell apart. Chloe at last had her share of pleasure, after years of baffling neglect. For the Vinssé brothers, it was like discovering a promised land. Their passion and joy were so intense that we often worried they would collapse under the weight of so much happiness. We'd never experienced this with Dr. Mars, or with Pierre Peloup or Myriam de Choiseul or Marjorie, who although wholehearted in their enjoyment of pleasure — they were all ex-tremely passionate — expressed their satisfaction with more reserve. The Vinssé brothers' howls would ring out along the banks of the clear canal, under the tall poplars, and if they withdrew for a moment, it was to come straight back in, not knowing where to look, or lick, or touch. We had to use threats to calm them down.

Chloe found them particularly to her liking. Perhaps she'd been waiting for them all this time to bring out her gaiety, her appetite for life? Whenever we were a bit worn out after satisfying them over and over again and were balking at the prospect of returning back along the canal, Chloe would offer to go with them alone. At times like this, when she showed herself to be strong-willed and determined, we didn't know who she most resembled. "Your father," said Marjorie. "Your mother, of course," said Dr. Mars, gallantly. Pierre Peloup was furious to learn that his territory by the canal had been colonized. For three days, we scoured the countryside together, looking for a spot equally well suited to our trysts. We needed somewhere with no houses nearby and a clear view to the horizon, so that we could make out the silhouette of a passerby or a car approaching. A number of times we met—in his gray sedan—in an open field in the middle of a huge plain. While we were going about our business, I could glimpse in the distance, whenever I raised my head, the two black spires of a cathedral. And for the first time I felt something stirring in me. Not love, that was still a long way off, young as I was, and in any case in a quite impossible situation; but the seed of love, a glimmer of hope, a first pang of grief for something higher, finer, more mysterious than our familial pleasures, which were neither high nor fine nor mysterious, but weren't the opposite of that either. Something broad, smooth, glacial, and imposing.

XIII

WITH THE ARRIVAL OF THE VINSSÉ BROTHERS, order was restored to our family. The rumormongering ceased, or people kept it to themselves at least. On the rue Alban-Berg, we no longer saw the neighbors across the way peeking through the curtains at us. People stopped snubbing us when we passed them in the street, and Papa could go out dressed as a woman again—only now he would walk up to the corner as a man and change clothes elsewhere.

For our mother, on the other hand, the blow inflicted by those two months of abstinence and caution may well have been fatal. She was truly ill from that point on, and when Dr. Mars came over, it wasn't simply to cheer her up or to celebrate the beauty of the great frozen lake of our dining-room table with her, but to examine her and prescribe her medicine, urge her to shake off her despondency and pull herself together. "Come, Marianne!" he would say, "you used to be so cheerful, so breathless for life, you were so radiant when you welcomed me into your backside, and you always wanted more! What's going on? Get a grip on yourself! Everything's back to normal, the children are happy, I can stop by between each house call, no one is preventing you from living your life exactly as you please." And since he was fond of flowery language, he added, "When, pray, will your dark and creamy behind smile on me once more?" Maman laughed, which wasn't like her at all.

Papa, who as I've already said had always been rather brutal with her, no longer cast so much as a glance in her direction. He would shut himself away with the insurance agent and Ingrid, sometimes having Chloe and me take part as well. We didn't really like the insurance agent—we thought he had a funny smell. Ingrid thought so, too, but she rather liked it. During the whole time Maman was ill—sad, that's to say—Papa didn't once set foot in the dining room. The sight of Maman was so hateful to him apparently that he would sometimes slam the dining-room door shut behind him, something he had never done before. Typically, he would close the door to his study, and once in a great while that of their bedroom; but the dining-room door that opened onto the tiled hall, never. Our "intimate household traffic," as the social worker would have called it, had been disrupted. To communicate with Maman, we had to sneak through the half-open door, closing it quietly behind us as soon as we were through; or alternatively, reduced to watching her swoon with pleasure—for she still fell into swoons—we would stand outside and eye her through the little window that gave onto the garden.

Marjorie was alarmed, more so than she had reason to be, no doubt. What she feared more than anything, I think, was that she would no longer be able to enjoy our company as often as she had in the past. I could sense this from a certain feverishness in her caresses, an unwonted zeal, the curious jealousy she displayed toward Pierre Peloup and the Vinssé brothers. Until then, our ties with the latter had served only to fan the flames of her love for Maman, of her often as not thwarted desire for Papa, of the intensity of her passion for Ingrid. "I'm unwanted! I can tell I'm a third wheel!" Marjorie would cry, regardless of the situation, even when we were in the midst of forming with her and Maman the most graceful figures, as they say in Sade—the really exciting ones, that is, the ones most conducive to pleasure. "Be nice to Marjorie," Maman would counsel us. Before adding, as if surprised by the thought: "I think she's hurting."

Dr. Mars, who was sensitive to suffering, or well-placed to alleviate it at any rate, withdrew from Maman's backside for a moment to do the honors of

Marjorie's. But it was obvious that Marjorie Higgins was less to his liking, perhaps because she was a brunette, perhaps because she didn't burn with the same insane passion as Maman, or perhaps because it was Maman and not Marjorie who was queen of the dining room, with its shining disc in which Dr. Mars would see his own reflection when he bent across it.

XIV

AS I LAY OUT THE BROAD STROKES OF OUR family life, I wouldn't want to give a false impression of our mother. I can see only too well that I'm trying to circumscribe her form. Perhaps I'll be able to take a more nuanced approach as my story advances and the memories return, floating up to the surface of the shining disc of our table. In spite of the years—which haven't overlaid all these impressions and emotions with "a thin pellicule of dust," as it says in the song, just shifted them about, so that all I have to do is reassemble them—our father, it seems, has always been a mystery to us. He was a mystery to begin with, and a mystery he has remained. Our mother, on the other hand, whose eyes I peer into wherever I happen to find myself—when watching the faces of actresses in films, or simply observing the faces of women everywhere—and whose erotic dispositions I scrutinize so as to see her at the center of her being, in that state of intense arousal where all is revealed—our mother was never a mystery to me. Or was so great a mystery, perhaps, that I wander at night in an unknown country whenever I approach her blinding form.

But what else do I have to name her by, if not her sex? She was so idle that it's impossible to connect her form to any activity outside her own home or family. She never left our sides. Until I was fifteen, the age at which I moved out, she never left us even for a second. We were the ones rushing back and forth, coming and going, bringing news of the outside world, but disclosing nothing of our domestic life except lies. She stayed indoors, in what we now know (it's one of the things Sade omits to mention) to be the "erotically charged" environment of the family home, going from her bedroom to the dining room, where she would consult the dark disc of the table, then back from the dining room to her bedroom again. Where else could she go? Papa's study was off-limits to her; when she came into the kitchen her mind was always occupied elsewhere; and she never spent long hours in the bathroom. She sewed, badly. She would invite Marjorie over, or Bénédicte, who took no part in our family life. She would occasionally pop out on an errand, but only once in a blue moon. We were the ones who brought back groceries for meals; Papa or Marjorie who took care of the other items of shopping.

She wasn't kept under lock and key by our father, who never tried to prevent her from going out. It was of her own free will that she stayed at the window, not even looking out at the garden. Her dresses? She would go out to buy clothes, but not more than two or three times a year. Books? She didn't read. "I have the demon of love in me," she would say. For she spoke well, much of the time like an oracle, and I've sometimes thought that, were I to place each of her phrases end to end, they'd make a book. To recover the words she spoke to us, however, I need to press her down against the frozen disc of the dining-room table, sometimes round, sometimes square, always mellow and always dark. It's an extraordinary experience, a quite dreadful one perhaps, and in order to go through with it, you have to make a show of levity, of gentle madness, at times. Netting the fleeting fish of reality is not easy; to catch them, a certain fecklessness—a certain forgetfulness even—is sometimes required.

I LEFT HOME AT FIFTEEN. I SET OUT WANdering at random and eventually wound up in a hotel in Normandy with a thousand francs in my pocket. I don't remember how I managed to end up there, in that particular hotel. My life ran along songlines like the ones in dreams. Even the shifts from one situation to the next had the same lack of logic you find in dreams. I was here and then I was there. How did I get from one to the other? I couldn't tell you.

In spite of that, I never had the feeling I was lost. On the contrary, it seemed to me that I knew very well who I was, where I was going and why, just as you do in dreams. And so I was safe from harm. People could tell I was determined, sure of myself, fearless. Alarming news reached me from home: "Mother frail. Permanently bedridden." "Mother delirious." "Mother dead." I didn't know what to make of all this in my new life.

For many years, I had no real feelings. Now that I'm nearing forty and, from time to time, by the grace of God, have felt a bit of tenderness here and there, a bit of affection even, I look back with curiosity on that age when I felt nothing besides my own strength.

I lied because I'd always lied. I made up other names for myself, other lives. I can remember telling a man who had picked me up hitchhiking that I was the daughter of a famous painter, because I'd seen a poster announcing an exhibition by that same famous painter. I covered my tracks so that I could be alone.

Yes, I will always deny that my childhood was traumatic. And it's not out of loyalty to my parents that I insist on the beauty of that period of my life. Our union was so intense and so compact, our sexual complicity so steadfast, like a firm handshake, that I've been leaning on it for support ever since, on the dark lake of our dining-room table. At no point has the past fallen from under my feet. And only once in my life have I lost my footing, for about two months, as if in a distant echo, decades later, of those two months of suspicions that kept us so cruelly separated from one another in our house on the rue Alban-Berg.

If I left my family early, it's because I was ready to lead my own life. But it took me a long time, I confess, to break the spell, to blow open the strongbox of my childhood and learn to feel affection. To walk out of the dream.

What may have helped me perhaps, compared to Ingrid and Chloe who have had more difficult lives than mine, was my taking it into my head to write stories. That was my handrail, a gleaming banister I could always cling to no matter how dark the night. I had a feel for words. They resonated for me; they had a presence, a profound consistency, they were almost creatures in their own right. My appetite for words was so pronounced that I enjoyed almost any book I read. I remember I read some bad ones when I ran off to Normandy for the first time, but I still found something in them to nourish me. It wasn't until later that my tastes grew more refined.

II

FUNNILY ENOUGH, GIVEN HOW GREGARIOUS our childhood had been—but perhaps too much so, and the cup was full—for many years I avoided any kind of sexual relationship. For a long time I was abstinent. At an age when young men and women start to quicken with new force, to shudder and rub themselves up against their peers, I was no more aware of my body than I was of my feelings. Only language tied me to my former life, which is perhaps why I took such pleasure in it.

Those were the years of long hitchhiking trips

from Normandy to Provence. Men would pick me up: red-headed men, dark-haired men with singsong accents, strange men, men in fast cars. Everything was an event for me because everything was beginning. I would inscribe the faces and behavior of these men in my mental notebooks: out of them I would build cathedrals like the one with the black spires I'd seen in the distance that day while Pierre Peloup was busying himself inside me and, for the first time, I'd had the idea of something higher and finer.

One man took me to Nevers, another to Nîmes, to another I said: "I'll go wherever you're going," then left him along the way. Another dropped me in a forest where yet another, on a bicycle this time, waved down cars for me, afraid I might lose my way.

I traveled with a family, I traveled with a man who was worried about me, and worried he might have a madwoman on his hands when I told him I was the daughter of a painter who'd been dead for a hundred years or more. I ended up on a beach where I sold some drawings I'd made. Where did I sleep? How did I pay for it all? I no longer remember. I think I was already managing to find rooms in cheap hotels located in respectable parts of town. It's a gift I've always had, at fifteen, at twenty, at twenty-five: finding a decent hotel with nothing to go on but my own intuition, something inexpensive, a godsend, always a godsend.

Meanwhile, more terrible news would reach me from home: "Father critically ill," "Father very weak." I was in a hotel when they announced: "Father dead." I can no longer remember whether it was the bells of the nearby church that I heard at that precise moment or bells that had started to ring furiously inside me. At all events, the news was accompanied by a great pealing of bells, a blue sky like the one Verlaine saw from the window of his cell, the feeling of something being born, a surge, a castle springing up inside me, with its towers, its crenellated walls, and its drawbridge raised.

III

AT THAT POINT IN MY LIFE, I WAS SEVENTEEN. My parents' premature deaths had left me the beneficiary of a small trust I could draw on once a month. It wasn't much. I think it came to two thousand francs. But it felt like a lot to me, since I never bought anything, stole the bare essentials I needed to live, made a habit of doing moonlight flits, and traveled without a ticket. I never felt poor, and no one would have thought to give me alms.

I wasn't sad to have lost my parents, since it opened up a space that, if anything, was bright and airy, like the sky in spring. I wrote regularly to my grandparents, sending them the kind of letters I knew would make them happy. Otherwise I was alone and free to act for myself.

Sometimes I try to recall what my body was like in those days, since that's where your impressions are stored, it's your body that sends its emotions out into the world. But I can't remember a thing. I don't think I ever once thought about pleasing people, ever once examined myself in a mirror or dreamed of asking myself if I were beautiful or not. My mind was too busy with other things. With what? And where? I couldn't say exactly, even if I had the sense that it mainly had to do with language.

A boy named Serge entered my life in the city of Arles, where I was staying. I wasn't smitten with him, but I did see him a handful of times. He was someone I could exchange a few words with. I continued, of course, to lie about my past, my name, what I liked and what I didn't like, but at least I had someone to lie to. And I needed that, since I hadn't spoken in so long that I was becoming a bit strange, and could be very aggressive at times. Serge was no fool; he knew that I was lying. He may even have found it rather attractive. Whenever he tried to fondle me or kiss me, I would shy away. Sometimes I grew weary of his psychologizing, which he insisted on sharing with me for my own enlightenment, perhaps because he wanted to help me, and definitely so that he would end up being able to fondle me. I put up with his theories with a yawn. When I listened to them, they always felt wrongheaded to me. But I owe it to Serge that I didn't become a complete stranger to myself and entirely alone, since he gave me, like a seed, a taste for meeting people, for conversation. And that was a beginning.

IV

MY SISTERS HAD MOVED OUT OF THE HOUSE on the rue Alban-Berg after my father's death. I waited until I was twenty before returning there. In the meantime another family had moved in, but they let me look round. Everything, of course, had changed, which was just as well. The hall had been painted white, the dining room had been converted into a living room, the study into a dining room, a huge kitchen had been built on, and the garden was less forbidding: it was blooming now, and shaded.

I found nothing. While I was taking tea with these people in the living room, Dr. Mars didn't once ring at the door, nor did Pierre Peloup's courageous mug appear at the window. Marjorie Higgins had long since gone mad.

Why is it that so many people in my life have wound

up insane? Couldn't they cling, like me, to the marvelous shining disc of the table, where our whole story is reflected? Couldn't they consult the table, make it speak and dance? Why did they neglect it? Wasn't it obvious to them, as it was to me, that this dark lake and its black waters would save us, so long as we kept peering down into it? Was it a bottomless well for all those who later lost their way? Did I love what I saw reflected there more than all the others did?

The visit put my mind at rest. It was a good thing, I told myself, that no trace remained of our past. But I couldn't help thinking about the table, I wanted to find it again. If there's one piece of furniture I would like to own, it's that enormous table, which was much too big to fit into my life. It was clearly a magic table, like the one in the Grimms' fairy tale where it says: "And when the time came for him to start on his travels, the carpenter gave him a little table. It was made of ordinary wood and there was nothing special about its appearance, but it had one excellent quality. If you put it down and said: 'Table, set yourself,' instantly a tablecloth would appear on the good little table, and on the tablecloth there would be a plate with a knife and fork beside it, and as many platters of roast meat and stewed meat as there was room for, and a big glass of the kind of red wine that rejoices the heart."

V

WHEN I WAS TWENTY, I SET OUT FOR
Pallanza, on Lake Maggiore. Here, there's another
gap in my memory: how did I end up choosing that
destination? True, there was a lake, but it wasn't
dark and shining like the one in our dining room,
although, if I look closely, there was that boat glid-
ing across the black water at night, silently, almost
like a ghost ship. It was sailing toward me, as if bringing me news. Would I have known how to interpret
that news? I don't think so. I could see that the boat
was laden with a revelation meant for me, but for a
long time I made no attempt to climb on board or
go belowdecks, and whenever I went on a day trip to
the Borromean Isles or crossed over to the opposite
shore of the lake, I did so only to make sure that the
hotel I was staying at in Pallanza, which I had found
without the help of a travel guide, without making
a reservation or even considering the alternatives,
was indeed the most agreeable in the entire region.
A godsend.

The hotel in Pallanza looked like a ship itself—
like a white steamship. It stood on the shore of the
lake, its somewhat dilapidated white facade lit up
by the sun. You came in through an enormous hallway covered with threadbare rugs, then you looked
up, and the four or five stories of the hotel climbed

all the way to a dome ringed by a gallery, leaving a large empty space in the middle. Naturally, I took the least expensive room, which was on the top floor. It cost a hundred and twenty francs, I think. I had told them I'd be spending a few weeks there, so when I went to pay my first bill after ten days, they turned me away. I could settle up later, when I checked out. They trusted me. Nevertheless, I remember paying out those first twelve hundred francs so as to keep my own affairs in order.

The room was small and sparse, with a single bed and a pinewood cupboard. There was a washstand with a mirror above it where I wrote *Ciao Luna! Ciao Rosa!* for the maids to find when I left. There was also a window leading onto a balcony where I would sit out with a chair and table to read and write. The balcony overlooked the lake.

So I saw it again at last, that shimmering dark surface! A surface you could lean across to examine the reflections that came from the sky, yet seemed to come from the depths of the lake itself. I spent a lot of time on that balcony, gazing out over the lake, especially in the evening when the sun began to set. I also spent a lot of time on boats, going from one island or one side of the lake to another, as if trying to encompass and contain, to examine from every conceivable point of view, this enormous table that was much too big for my life.

VI

I NO LONGER REMEMBER WHAT PROMPTED me to leave Pallanza. Probably I'd simply run out of money. Yet I seem to have left for Rome, since I can still see myself on an overnight train, seated opposite a matronly Italian woman eating a sausage, and a fat and very ugly French girl with her legs spread wide apart, pretending to sleep when she was manifestly trying to recruit the stranger seated across from her as a lover. I spread a scarf over my bare legs and began to fall asleep in turn. The matronly Italian woman gave me an approving smile.

In Rome, I met an old man, a composer. Strolling through the gardens of the Villa Borghese, he stopped in front of the bench I was seated on and invited me to come and have tea with him at his home. Marino Studi lived at the foot of the Palatine Hill. You had to climb the flight of steps to the Capitol, take a right through the alley leading down toward the Forum, and just below this was the four-story house where he lived, with a knocker on the door to announce your arrival. You knocked, the door opened, and his maid, mad Bruna, welcomed you in. "She says some funny things sometimes," Studi warned me. One day when we were talking about Socrates with a friend, she shouted: "It wasn't Socrates who said that! It was

Aristotle!" Bruna would smile at you with a know-ing, conspiratorial air as she plonked down onto the table the unfailingly inedible dishes she had cooked. I don't know how, but with Bruna I almost managed to chat in Italian, though I'd never learned the lan-guage. I remember the day she unpacked my bags, after Studi had invited me to stay there for a while. My suite, consisting of a bedroom with a vaulted ceil-ing and a green velvet bedspread, and a living room that overlooked the street, had once belonged to his sister. We weren't permitted to speak to him or to go upstairs to his rooms to say hello before three in the afternoon. Until then he practiced the yoga of sound, and of light, too, making the light circulate inside him. At three o'clock, I would go up and we'd set off for the beach together. On the beach I once saw him speak in Italian, French, and English with an old and very distinguished-looking woman. In the car, Studi, who would ride in the back with me, casually put a hand on my thigh. I didn't like that. I brushed it away. Before leaving the beach, he would salute the sun, joining his hands together and making a deep bow from the waist.

He would try repeatedly to force my modesty and my modesty would resist, but I rather liked living in his home. During the day, I explored Rome; in the evening, I dined alone with him in his salon. I was always taking issue with him and his ideas, or mocking him for his presumptuousness. But I felt comfortable with him, and more than comfortable with mad Bruna.

I wandered about Rome as I wandered everywhere during that blessed period of my life. I say blessed because it was then that I stored up the resources that would prove crucial in the years to come. It was as though I'd just been released from prison, everything was an event to me, and in certain respects I was so alone that nothing stood between me and the spectacle of the world. I was free to think, free to come and go as I pleased. I came upon people the way you come upon signs; I bound myself to none of them, yet each of them engraved themselves and their attributes in my memory, as though I was assembling a collection of gods. I remember a tiny, ancient man who lived on the outskirts of Rome, a happy soul with whom I ate cheese in the kitchen of a housing project. And another, well-to-do and also elderly, who invited me to dine with him on the terrace of a restaurant and whom I drank wine with for the first time in my life. And a third who, on a coach home from the Villa d'Este, slid an arm behind the shoulders of his girlfriend to stroke the back of my neck. I didn't have a penny, and still I lived like a queen, going from one *pensione* to another after I'd moved out of Studi's. Everything I saw filled me with an intense,

piercing pleasure, everywhere I went I found mean-
ingful phenomena on the march: a tree in bloom
and birds screeching outside the window of my
boardinghouse on the Aventino in May; in another
part of Rome, a boardinghouse with a dark, frozen
corridor like the hallway in my childhood home.

VII

IN ROME, I MET SOMEONE WHO WAS TO PLAY
a crucial role in my life. I passed a woman one morning on the Piazza del Popolo, and at the sight of her
I immediately felt a surge of lust, for the first time in
years. She was tall and blond, with her hair swept up
in a high bun. She stood very straight, wore a white
coat, and had slim legs and voluptuous breasts. My
quotidian existence evaporated the moment I set
eyes on her, and for three days I did nothing but
track her across the city. I had no desire to know
who she was, her name or her situation; I wanted
to know how she went about her life, whether she
was solitary or not, talkative or reserved, cheerful
or gloomy. I wanted to know what she did with her
days. She never took a bus or a taxi and would walk
long distances toward a destination I was never able
to identify. The first day, she walked up the Via del
Corso without stopping in front of a single boutique,

without peering into a single shop window, and went into a building at 72 Via Vittorio Emanuele II. I thought it must have been her home and waited on the nearest corner. But barely ten minutes later she reemerged, lost in thought, walking swiftly on without once turning round. She was heading in the direction of the Vatican, but instead of crossing the Tiber at the Castel Sant'Angelo, she veered off suddenly, continuing to walk at a brisk pace, never once glancing round or stopping. She reminded me of those flies that trace geometric patterns around a light bulb at high speed, weaving an invisible web, laying invisible threads, linking and meshing together parallelograms, trapezoids, triangles, like so many mathematical exercises or turns in a mental kaleidoscope. I could barely keep up.

She would vanish at nightfall. Not in some fantastical way like a ghost, but just as the sun was about to set, at the moment the street lamps were starting to come on, I would suddenly lose sight of her. The first evening, I put it down to some absentmindedness on my part. The second, I cursed myself for having let my concentration slip. On the third I understood that she simply vanished at that twilight hour when the world turns abruptly on its axis, and that there was nothing to be done about it. I came home disappointed, annoyed that I hadn't been able to follow my quest to its end. But one morning, when I had gone to Cinecittà to make some money working as an extra, I found her again.

VIII

SHE WAS APPEARING IN THE SAME FILM. That's how I managed to approach her and speak to her. She was half-French and cocked her head at me, obviously amused, smoking cigarette after cigarette, though it must be said in a very elegant manner, as if each of her cigarettes just happened to be there, by chance, in her pocket. Her name was Leonella. "You're alone?" she said. "A pretty girl like you!" And she laughed.

She wasn't much of a conversationalist, but I loved her. Maybe because she was more mature than I was: she told me one day that she was thirty-two. She seemed to be perfectly at home in her body, treating it with a familiarity and friendliness that I found captivating. I can see her now, waiting for the call that would summon her to the set, dangling her long tanned legs over a little wall on the backlot and dragging on her nth cigarette. She'd exhale and arch her back to tug at her dress where it stuck to her thighs and waist, taking another greedy drag with her head thrown back. Then she'd look up at the sky, and groan:

"Christ, it's taking forever! If there's one thing I really hate, it's the movies! I could never be an actress!"

"Then why are you here?" I asked, squatting on the ground in front of her like a child watching a puppet show.

She shrugged. "You have to make a living somehow!" she said, exactly like the heroine of a B movie.

"Leonella," I said, "you're so beautiful, you could be an incredible actress. A star! Like Anita Ekberg in *La Dolce Vita*."

She looked at me, laughing behind the curtain of smoke from her cigarette.

"And what about you? You want to be an actress?"

"Oh no, I'm just trying to make enough money to stay alive."

"Then what do you want to be?" she asked. "You're such a queer little fish."

"A writer, perhaps," I said, something I'd never confessed to anyone except Chloe. "But I'm not sure I really have what it takes; I mean, sometimes I'm sure that I do, and sometimes I'm terrified that I could ever have bought into such a pipe dream."

We wound up living together. And when I say "wound up," it all happened quite fast. The second day of the shoot she invited me to move in with her.

"I'm alone and bored, and you're sweet and you make me laugh. Come and stay for a while and then we'll see how it goes."

I wanted Leonella but I didn't know if she wanted me, or if she even knew how I felt about her. There was something about her that was so dreamy and haphazard and unintentional, and so totally unlike me, that it was hard for me to understand her.

"You should dress differently," she told me, "you don't show yourself to your best advantage. And you're a bit on the plump side, too — you should lose a little weight."

In a fortnight I became slim and almost pretty. In the room where Leonella lived on Via Boncompagni, I said to her, still in awe, "You're such a mystery. Have you ever been married? I'd swear you have a child hidden away somewhere. To me, you're like a character in a novel."

She shrugged. "Enough of your nonsense. And come on you, you need to spend more time in your body! You're so ... so ... abstract!"

And for months we laughed at that "abstract," the term she had used the first night I came to her place. "Ab Stracht, not a bad name for a writer," she said. "You should use it." Together we imagined my novels to come: *Leonella in Love* by Ab Stracht. *Leonella and Her Friend* by Ab Stracht.

She lived poorly enough but she certainly hadn't always been poor: she had well-cut clothes and some antique jewelry, a pretty handbag, and a few other things in very good taste.

"You've had a tidy, bourgeois existence," I said, "then there was some unspeakable drama, and now you suffer this reversal of fortune nobly. That's how I see you."

Leonella laughed.

"You really are nuts, but I love you."

IX

WE NEVER HAD ENOUGH MONEY AND NEEDED desperately to earn some, so we seldom left Rome. But one day we went to the gardens of the Villa d'Este, and that was where Leonella revealed herself to me at last. Not her body, which I'd embraced and held tight against my own through so many nights, nor the spectacular vision of her naked form, of which I'd had my fill over the past three months, while she stood soaping herself at the washbasin, or slept pressed against me, while I caressed her, as if I'd become a man. None of that had stirred a thing in me.

At the Villa d'Este, she climbed up the stone steps and I followed behind her. I was sad to have brought her to those gardens, sad to have spent more than three hours there without finding anything new in either her or me, when all of a sudden I saw her white coat replaced by a white dress, her blond hair changed to someone else's, and I was transported at a stroke to the mirrored hall, and from there onto the black, shining table, and felt then, to my great surprise, a despair so violent that it was like an earthquake in my heart, as if its two halves had been pulled apart, shredded and torn asunder, as if that was what had really happened in our house on the rue Alban-Berg without my ever realizing it, as if that table, instead of being a thing of joy and of frenzied, passionate delight, had been a sacrificial altar, as if I'd been amputated there, tortured and dismembered, but back then had somehow dreamed my way through it all.

WHEN I ARRIVED BACK FROM ROME, I DIS-
covered that my older sister Ingrid had gotten married. For the first time, her life was no longer spent
wandering back and forth, somber and secretive, as
it had been ever since she'd left home.

I remember the visit I paid her, one day in early
spring. At the sound of the bell at the front gate she
appeared on the porch, so pretty and fresh in a short,
orange summer frock that it was like experiencing
spring twice over. Her arms were sleek and tan, her
smile was peaceful. She was holding an infant who
was chewing gently on the fabric of her dress. It was
the first baby in our family, the first success.

"How are you?" Ingrid asked, walking toward me
through the timidly flowering garden. She was almost worldly, affable, freed from the nets that for so
long had held her captive. And we sat ourselves down

in the garden, next to the wall of the house, while behind us in the wide-open ground-floor windows the pink cotton curtains billowed and flapped in the breeze.

I had a nephew, then, whom I scrutinized with interest. Nearby, a long garden hose made of bright green rubber snaked across the gravel. Further on, the sides of a metal basin reflected the blinding light of the sun. There were small children running here and there, because Ingrid made her living as a babysitter. Her husband was working in the garden behind the house.

"You'll see him at lunch," she said.

Was our life going to become simple, peaceful and happy at last? Finding myself next to a married Ingrid was like being presented with a map, a landscape I could smooth out on a table with the flat of my hand. All the bumpy, tortuous roads that the folds of the crumpled paper had partially or completely obscured now appeared plainly traced out, winding peacefully through the countryside. And it was the same for the lakes and mountains, the coastal regions and the cities: everything was clearly pinpointed, clearly named, so that you could see exactly how to get from one village to another, or from this plain to that shore. You could calculate the precise distance and how much time you would need to make the journey, and each name on the map corresponded to a shape or symbol, each shape or symbol to a name. You knew where you were.

She held slightly aloof as she spoke, brushing aside any allusion to our childhood, driving the images of the past conjured up by my presence far behind her the moment they arose and leaving them to implode in the shadows. She nattered on about my new haircut, about her son, her pregnancy, the labor and the delivery, the work her husband did in the garden, then again about her son, again about the labor and the delivery, her husband and the garden, without once leaving a gap in which our eyes might meet and address the question that was written there, a question so serious and profound that it would have been terrifying to have to confront it: "How are you?"

I played along, feigning an interest in the pregnancy, the garden, her husband's planting. Ingrid knew I was playing along. And she also knew I would play along for as long as she wanted. She let me see she knew and thanked me for it, a little at a time, prudently, with a few seconds of silence in the flood of words or a brief relaxation of the tension in her limbs. "No," I said silently. My eyes, my whole body said, "No, Ingrid, you have nothing to be afraid of, I won't mention the past, I won't bring up anything from our past." "Thank you," said her body, then the body of the baby she held in her arms, "thank you."

And her deep dark eyes, open onto the night within, said: "Let's not speak about that. You know we need to live somehow." And so we returned to her pregnancy, the baby, her husband's gardening, my new haircut.

We didn't go round in circles. No. On the contrary. We wove a little net in which our exhausted bodies could find rest. We toiled blindly, one behind the other, for my part in the most conscientious fashion, setting the tone, as it were, defining a form, a structure whose chief characteristic was simply to be alive, to reach out to life, to secure and uphold it.

II

I LEFT INGRID'S HOUSE WITH A NEW DROP of peace in my heart. I've always loved traveling by train. The return journey, when I had to change trains three times, is one of the most beautiful memories I possess. For one of the connections, I remember, I had to wait two hours. With Ingrid I had secretly unfolded the map of our life on a dark table and, for the first time perhaps, had been able to make out clearly the layout of the roads and the lay of the land, so I awaited my train in the station buffet with confidence. Everything seemed to be in its proper place: the waiter wiping glasses behind the bar, the passengers disembarking, the lost souls stopping in for a drink. Even the conversations I overheard seemed somehow right, exactly as they should have been. The world took on a spellbinding clarity.

Giddy with it all, I went for a short walk in town. The streets were empty—it was a Sunday—so I walked as far as the church, which turned out to be a cathedral whose black spires sent me hurtling back into my extraordinary childhood. And I realized that they were the same spires I had seen when Pierre Peloup, in his stationary, silver-gray sedan, in the middle of an enormous plain, was busying himself on top of me, inside me, beneath me, while I observed a bird on the other side of the car door, and Marianne, my mother, on fire with lust, waited for a visitor to call. And I saw that everything was right with the world, that it laughs as it traces its loops and spirals, and that you only had to pay—as I had always known and believed—close attention for a terrible joy to be born in your life, for a work of art to be forged from your body, your hands, your eyes, your poor broken heart.